# The Usborne SCIENCE FUN

M. Johnson,
J.G. McPherson, A. Ward
Illustrated by Colin King

## Contents

# Flight and floating

Flight and Floating was written by A. Ward
Chemistry Experiments was written by M. Johnson
Fun with electronics was written by J. G. McPherson

Science Consultants: Dr M. P. Hollins and M. Owen
Editors: Helen Davies and Lisa Watts

First published in 1981 by Usborne Publishing Ltd, Usborne House, 83-85 Saffron Hill, London EC1N 8RT, England.

Copyright © 1992, 1988, 1981 Usborne Publishing Ltd

Printed in Great Britain

We are grateful to John Murray (Publishers) Ltd for permission to reproduce Barnaby's glider (pages 28–31) from "How to make and fly paper aircraft" by Barnaby.

This part of the book is full of experiments to help you find out how things fly and float. There are lots of models to make too, and ideas for testing them to see how they work. The first part is about flight and the second about floating.

With each model or experiment there is an explanation to show how it works. You can find out how real things, such as submarines and helicopters, work too.

Over the page there is a list of the main things you need for the models and experiments and some hints on how to make them successful.

There are lots of puzzles to do, which you can solve by experimenting. You can check your results with the answers on page 61.

3

# Being a scientist

When you build a model, or do an experiment, you need to be careful and accurate, as a real scientist would be. On these two pages there are some hints on being a scientist. If you follow these, your projects should be successful, though even real scientists sometimes have to repeat experiments because they do not work first time.

It is a good idea to start collecting equipment. You can find most of the things you need around the house. Put them in an old box, or if you have a shed, you could make it your "laboratory".

USEFUL THINGS

PAPER
PENCIL
RULER
FELT-TIP PEN
SCISSORS
STICKY TAPE
GLUE
PLASTICINE
CANDLE

DRINKING STRAW
PAPER-CLIPS
STRING
COTTON REELS
EMPTY PLASTIC BOTTLE
NAILS
JAM JARS

## Getting ready

Collect everything you need before you start. If you do not have one thing, try and think of something else you can use.

USE BOTH HANDS TO MAKE FOLDS

When you are making models, measure or trace lines accurately. Be especially careful to make folds smooth and even.

## Hints for doing tests

**1**

Set tests up carefully, as the conditions in the room can affect the results. Make sure draughts do not spoil flight tests and that water is deep enough for floating.

**2**

Before you do an experiment, try to guess what will happen. Then you can do the experiment to see if your idea was right. Do not look at the explanation first.

**3**

Watch tests closely. Sometimes things will happen very quickly, so you have to concentrate hard. Repeat a test several times to be sure the result is not a fluke.

**4**

If your results are different from those in the book, it does not mean they are wrong. See if you can work out what happened and then try some tests to check your idea.

### Finding out more

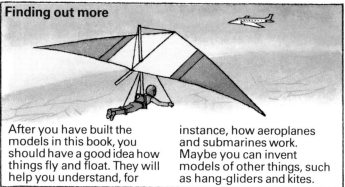

After you have built the models in this book, you should have a good idea how things fly and float. They will help you understand, for instance, how aeroplanes and submarines work. Maybe you can invent models of other things, such as hang-gliders and kites.

# Falling and floating

The experiments on this page are about falling. Things fall because they are pulled towards the Earth by a force called gravity.

You can find out more about gravity by doing the test on the right.

You can find out more about gravity by doing the test on the right.

## 1 Gravity test

Screw up a piece of paper and find a heavy stone. Drop both from the same height, at the same moment, and note when they land.

The ball of paper lands at the same time as the stone, even though it is much lighter. This is because the effect of gravity is the same on all objects, no matter how heavy.

## Another way of falling

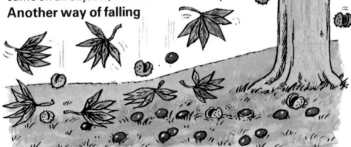

Have you ever watched falling leaves and conkers, though, on a still day? The conkers fall straight to the ground, but the leaves float down slowly. Can you think why this should be?

6

## Experiment

Take two pieces of paper and crumple one into a ball, as you did before.

Drop them from the same height, at the same moment, and watch when they land.

Try it several times. Why do you think the flat paper always falls more slowly?

## Why it happens

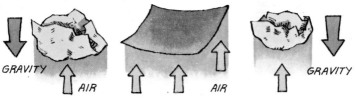

As the papers fall, air is trapped and squashed under them. This air presses up against them and stops them falling so fast. The flat paper falls more slowly than the crumpled one because it has a larger area, so more air is trapped underneath it. This is also why the large, flat leaves fall more slowly than the conkers.

## Trick your friends

Tear two pages from a notebook, and write the word "HEAVY" on one. Ask some friends if they can work out how to drop the papers from the same height, at the same time, and make the "HEAVY" one land first. (Answer: crumple the "HEAVY" paper so it traps less air.)

7

# Making parachutes

The modern parachute was invented in 1797 by André–Jacques Garnerin. He jumped out of a hot air balloon and, wearing his parachute, floated safely to the ground. His daughter, Eliza, was the first woman parachutist.

To make some paper parachutes, you need tissue paper, sticky tape, thread and paper-clips.

To make two parachutes, one slightly larger than the other, cut two squares of tissue paper, one 30cm×30cm and one 20cm×20cm.

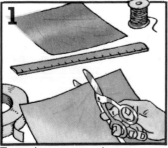

Tape threads, about 15cm long, to each corner of each piece of paper.

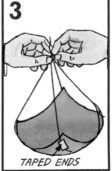

*TAPED ENDS*

Tie the threads like this, with the taped ends on the outside of the parachute.

Hook two paper-clips on to each parachute, so both have an equal load.

## How parachutes work

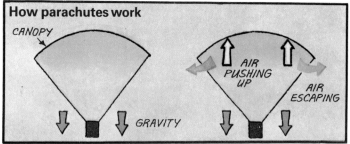

Gravity pulls the parachute down, but as it falls, air is trapped under the canopy. The air gets squashed up or compressed, and pushes up against the canopy, making the parachute fall slowly.

**5**

To test the parachutes, drop them from the top of the stairs, or stand on a chair. Why do you think one of the parachutes takes longer to fall? See what happens if you hook on more paper-clips.

## Experiment

The trapped air escapes unevenly from under the canopy, and makes the parachute sway. Try cutting a hole in the top, to see if it helps to stop this.

### Garnerin's parachute

Garnerin's parachute wobbled badly as the trapped air escaped in sudden spurts from either side of the canopy. This made him feel very sick, so he made a hole in the top of the canopy to let the air escape more smoothly. All modern parachutes have a hole at the top.

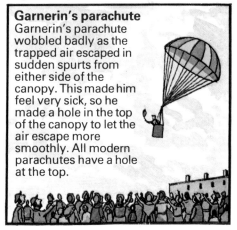

# Paper helicopters

These two pages show you how to make a paper helicopter. Then, over the page, there are some helicopter experiments and a game to play.

Cut a piece of paper so it measures 20cm×7cm. Then make three cuts in it, as shown.

*FOLD*   *BEND*

Fold over the two sides below the cuts, to make a thin strip. Bend the end of the strip up.

Fold the two strips at the top out as shown, to make the rotors which make the helicopter spin.

### Flight test
Now stand on a chair and drop the helicopter. Watch how it takes a second or two to start spinning.

### Puzzles
1. Can you make another helicopter, out of the same sized paper, which falls more quickly? You will need to alter the design slightly (Answer on page 61.)
2. How can you make the helicopter spin round the other way? You can find out in the explanation on the opposite page, but try to work it out first.

## Why the helicopter spins

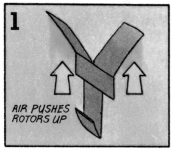

**1** AIR PUSHES ROTORS UP

As the paper helicopter falls, air is trapped under the rotors. The pressure of the air pushes the rotors up in a slanting position.

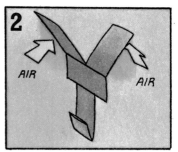

**2** AIR AIR

In this position, the air under one rotor is pushing one way and the air under the other rotor is pushing the opposite way.

**3** HELICOPTER SPINNING AS IT FALLS

Now, as the helicopter falls, the two forces of air push the rotors round and make it spin.

**4**

Try bending the rotors back in the opposite direction and see what happens.

**5**

Now the forces of air push the other way and the helicopter spins in the opposite direction.

### Flying top
Spinning keeps the helicopter upright and stops it toppling over as it falls. In the same way, a spinning top can balance on its end.

11

## Paper helicopter experiments

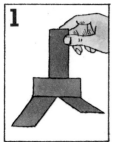

**1** Try dropping a paper helicopter upside-down. Does it turn up the right way again?

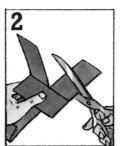

**2** What happens if you cut off half of one of the rotors?

**3** Now cut one rotor off completely. Do you think the helicopter will still spin?

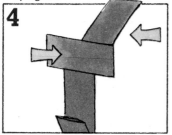

**4** Watch carefully how it falls. Air presses against the base of the rotor, so there are still two forces of air making it spin.

**5** What happens if you cut the base of the rotor off too? Can you think of other tests to try out on the helicopter?

### Sycamore helicopters

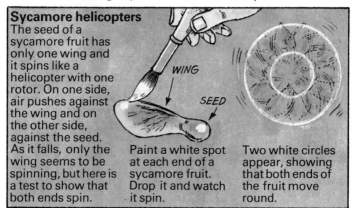

The seed of a sycamore fruit has only one wing and it spins like a helicopter with one rotor. On one side, air pushes against the wing and on the other side, against the seed. As it falls, only the wing seems to be spinning, but here is a test to show that both ends spin.

WING

SEED

Paint a white spot at each end of a sycamore fruit. Drop it and watch it spin.

Two white circles appear, showing that both ends of the fruit move round.

## Helicopter game

For this game you need to make a target as shown below and some helicopters. Then take it in turns to bomb the target. You can make up your own rules, or use these: score two points for a bull's eye, one for inside the circle, and lose one if you miss altogether.

BULL'S EYE

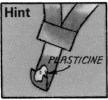

### Hint

PLASTICINE

If no-one can hit the bull's eye, try weighting each helicopter with a small piece of plasticine.

### Making the target

Put a large plate on a big piece of paper and draw round it to make a circle.

For the bull's eye, put a cup in the middle of the circle.

Make three helicopters for each player.

# Vertical take-off helicopter

Try making this helicopter
which lifts itself up off a
launching pad.

You need a piece of card about
20cm × 20cm (the back of a
cereal packet would do), tracing
paper, pencil, ruler, paper-clips
and a thin, plastic cotton reel.

For the launching pad you need
a stick, such as a paintbrush
handle, narrow enough to slip
through the cotton reel, and
some string.

# How to make the helicopter

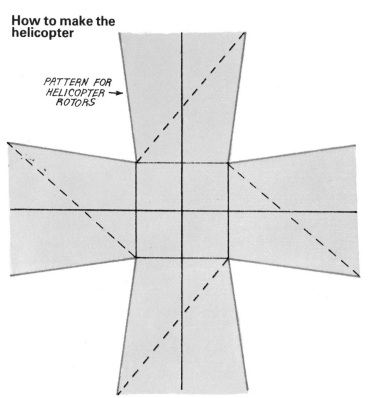

PATTERN FOR
HELICOPTER →
ROTORS

You must have this pattern the right way round, so trace it, then scribble on the back of the tracing. Put it the right way up on the centre of the card, then draw over the lines again.

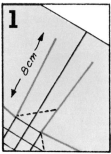

Extend the red lines until they each measure 8cm.

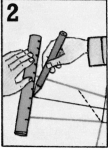

Join the tops of the red lines to make the rotors.

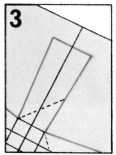

Now each rotor should look like this.

15

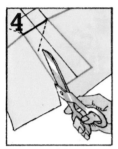

**4**

Cut round the rotors following the lines carefully.

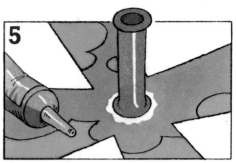

**5**

Turn the card over and glue the cotton reel in the middle where the rotors meet. Use a strong, all-purpose glue and leave it to dry for a few hours so it is firmly stuck.

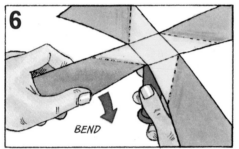

**6**

BEND

Bend the rotors down along the dotted lines, as shown. This is very important – it makes the rotors slant, so one edge is lower than the other. Take care not to break the card.

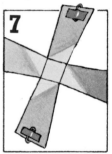

**7**

Tape paper-clips to the ends of two rotors which are opposite each other.

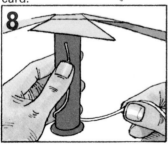

**8**

Now wind the string round the cotton reel. Hold one end along the reel, to catch it in, and start winding from the bottom.

**9**

UPPER EDGE

WIND THIS WAY

Make sure you wind the string so it goes round towards the upper edge of each rotor. It should go round 15 times.

# Lift off

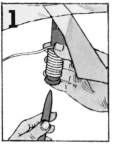

Holding the string tight, put the cotton reel on to the end of the stick.

Hold the stick in one hand and the string in the other, as shown.

**3**

Then pull the string firmly and steadily, until it comes right off the reel. The helicopter should spin up into the air. You can find out how it works on the next page.

## Launching hints

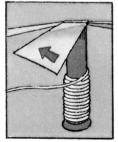

Make sure you have wound the string towards the upper edge of each rotor.

Check that the rotors are bent down properly.

Try slanting the stick slightly, and make sure you do not jerk the string.

# How a helicopter takes off

Your model helicopter takes off in a similar way to a real one. On both, the rotors spinning round lift the helicopter into the air. The rotors are driven round by the engine on a real helicopter. On the model, you pull the string to make them spin.

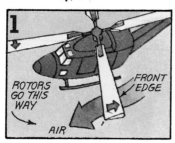

Helicopter rotors are slanted, so the front edge is higher than the back. As they turn, the front edge cuts into the air and forces it down under the back edge.

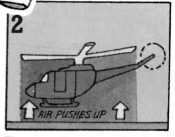

The more the rotors spin, the more air is pushed down and the pressure of the air under the rotors pushes the helicopter up.

18

## Steering a helicopter

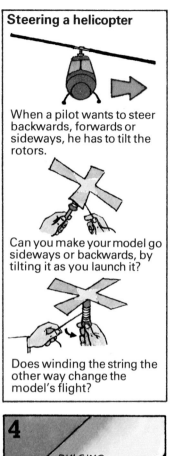

When a pilot wants to steer backwards, forwards or sideways, he has to tilt the rotors.

Can you make your model go sideways or backwards, by tilting it as you launch it?

Does winding the string the other way change the model's flight?

**3**

The rotors of the model are bent so they work in the same way. Air is pressed down and the increased pressure under the model pushes it up into the air.

**4**

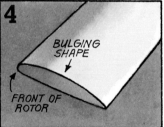

BULGING SHAPE

FRONT OF ROTOR

Helicopter rotors are a special bulging shape and this also helps them to fly. You can find out about this on page 34.

19

# How to make paper fly

On these two pages you can find out how to make a sheet of paper into a simple glider. You need a piece of paper about 20cm×25cm.

First see what happens if you drop the paper flat, like this. It sways from side to side and may even flip right over. You need to find a way to make it glide forward and fall smoothly.

**2**

20 cm EDGE

Fold the paper in half as shown. Then open it out and drop it as before. The crease should stop it swaying from side to side.

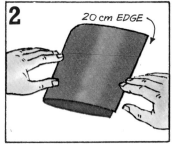

**3**

MAKE SURE FOLD IS NEAT AND EVEN

To make it go forward, try making one end heavier. Fold one long edge back about 1.5cm. Drop the paper again.

**4**

Keep folding the edge over, 1.5cm at a time, and testing the paper until the front edge is heavy enough and the paper glides forward.

## What is happening

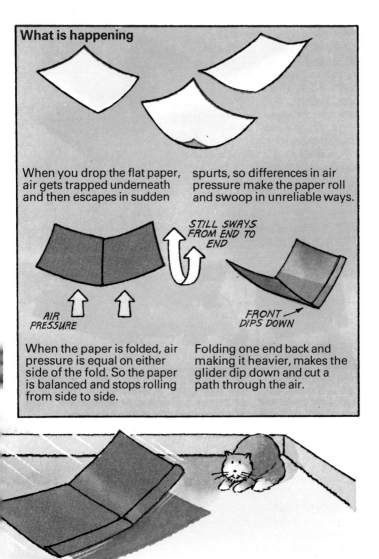

When you drop the flat paper, air gets trapped underneath and then escapes in sudden spurts, so differences in air pressure make the paper roll and swoop in unreliable ways.

STILL SWAYS FROM END TO END

AIR PRESSURE

FRONT DIPS DOWN

When the paper is folded, air pressure is equal on either side of the fold. So the paper is balanced and stops rolling from side to side.

Folding one end back and making it heavier, makes the glider dip down and cut a path through the air.

If you fold the paper too many times the glider will dive sharply because the front is too heavy. If you do not fold it enough, the glider will lurch up and down. Keep experimenting until the weight is right and it glides smoothly.

# Glider flight research

Here are some tests to find
out how to control the glider
on page 20 and make it
fly in the direction you
want. To do this you
need flaps, called
elevons, in the back
edge. You can find out
how to cut them below.

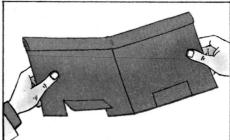

ELEVON
FLAPS

It is best to do the tests in a
room with no draughts, as these may blow the glider off
course. Close doors and windows and keep away from
heaters which create air currents. Clear an open space so the
glider does not crash into things.

## How to make elevons

2cm

Fold the glider in
half and make two
cuts, 2cm deep and
5cm apart as shown.

Open the glider out and bend one elevon
up. To test the glider, hold it in both hands
and drop it. Then see what happens if you
bend up the other elevon instead.

## How elevons work

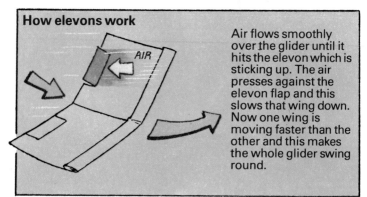

AIR

Air flows smoothly
over the glider until it
hits the elevon which is
sticking up. The air
presses against the
elevon flap and this
slows that wing down.
Now one wing is
moving faster than the
other and this makes
the whole glider swing
round.

## Flight tests

Now see how many different directions you can make the glider fly in. The glider works best if you launch it instead of dropping it, and you can find out how to do that here.

### How to launch

### How to hold the glider

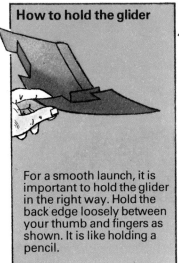

For a smooth launch, it is important to hold the glider in the right way. Hold the back edge loosely between your thumb and fingers as shown. It is like holding a pencil.

Hold the glider at shoulder height and, aiming slightly downwards, push it gently into the air. If it does not work very well at first you are probably pushing too hard.

### Aerobatic puzzles

You can make the glider do all sorts of things by bending the elevons up or down and launching it at different angles.

See if you can work out how to make it do the following:
1. Loop the loop.
2. Dive and turn upside-down.
3. Turn sharply left or right.

(Answers on page 61.)

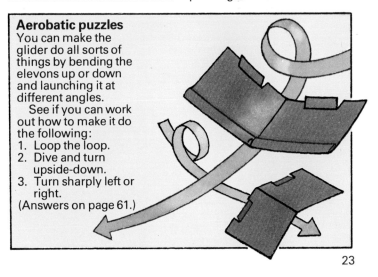

# Mark 2 glider

Here is another glider to make. It has wings and a tail, like an aeroplane. There are two sets of control flaps, one on the wings and one on the tail. These do the same job as elevons, but in a different way.

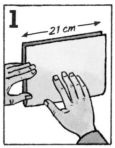

Fold in half a sheet of paper measuring at least 21cm×30cm, as shown here.

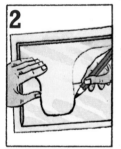

Trace the pattern on page 62 on to one side of the folded paper.

Cut round the pattern through both thicknesses of paper, and cut the slits too.

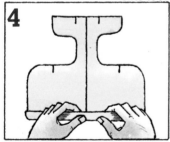

Then open the paper out and fold the front edge back 1.5cm. Test it, and keep on folding and testing it until it flies smoothly.

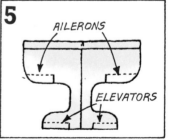

Now fold back the edges of the wings and tail to make flaps. The wing flaps are ailerons and the tail flaps are elevators.

24

## Making the glider turn

Ailerons make the glider turn left or right. See what happens if you bend the left one up and the right one down. Then try them the other way round.

## Climbing and diving

Elevators make the glider dive or climb. What happens when you bend both up and drop the glider nose first?

Then try bending both elevators down and launching the glider horizontally.

Over the page you can find out how flight controls work.

## How elevators work

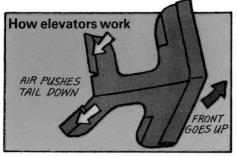

AIR PUSHES TAIL DOWN

FRONT GOES UP

AIR PUSHES UP

When both elevators are up, air trapped against them pushes the glider's tail down. This makes the front go up and so the glider climbs.

When both elevators are down, air pushes the tail up and the glider dives.

## How ailerons work

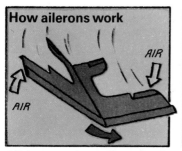

AIR

AIR

Ailerons work together to make the glider turn. Trapped air pushes the wing with the raised flap down and the other wing up. This tilts the glider and makes it swing round. When the left flap is up it turns to the left. It turns right with the right one up.

## How aeroplanes turn

TAIL PLANE

RUDDER

To turn, aircraft use a tail flap called the rudder, as well as ailerons. To turn right, the rudder is bent right. Air pressing against it pushes the tail to the left and the plane swings round to the right. The ailerons make the plane tilt as it turns. This is called banking and it helps the plane to turn.

# High-speed flight controls

Planes which are designed for high-speed flight, such as *Concorde,* have special triangular-shaped wings. They are called delta wings after the Greek letter "delta" which is written like this △.

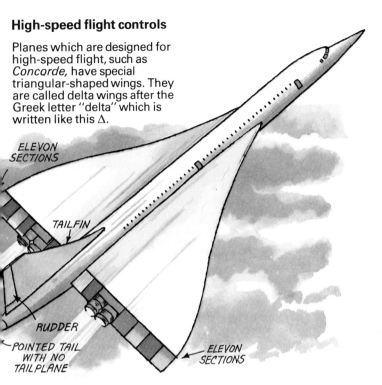

ELEVON SECTIONS

TAILFIN

RUDDER

POINTED TAIL WITH NO TAILPLANE

ELEVON SECTIONS

Delta-winged aircraft have a tailfin, but no tailplane, so they cannot have separate ailerons and elevators. Instead they have elevons, like the glider on page 22, which do the job of both. *Concorde* has three elevon sections on each wing.

## Using elevons

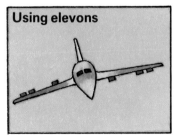

To make the plane bank for a turn, the elevons are raised on one side and lowered on the other, like ailerons.

To climb and turn right, the rudder is bent right and the right elevons raised. The left ones are kept level.

# Make and fly a superglider

In 1967 a "Great International Paper Airplane Competition" was held in America. One of the winning gliders was made by Ralph Barnaby. He used to make paper gliders while on ballooning trips in the 1920s, and test them by dropping them from the balloon. Often he could see them circling below for 20 minutes before they disappeared from sight. Here is a glider, like Barnaby's winner, for you to make.

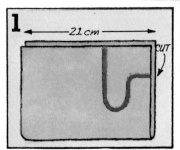

You need a piece of paper measuring 21cm×30cm, folded as shown. Draw a pattern on it, like the one here, and cut it out.

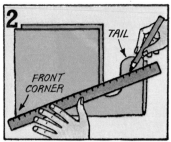

Place a ruler over the front corner and across the tail like this. Draw a line on the tail only, as shown in the picture.

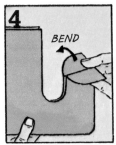

Bend out one side of the tail along the line you have drawn.

Bend out the other side in the same way, using the first fold as a guide.

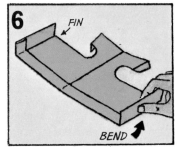

Open the glider out and fold back the front edge, like this, until the wings are about half their original size.

Bend up about 2cm at the tip of each wing, to make "fins". These help to keep the glider on a straight course.

## Test flight

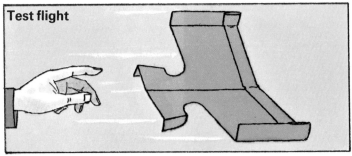

Now test the superglider, launching it as shown for the glider on page 23.

If it does not fly very well you can find out how to improve it over the page.

## Improving the superglider

Here are some ways to improve the glider if
it does not fly very well at first.

**1. If the glider dives**
Try cutting elevators*
in the tail and
bending them up.

**2. If it still dives**
The front is too heavy. Try
folding the front edge back less.
Or you may have to make a new
glider, with a broader wing.

**3. If it lurches up and down**
It may help to cut a thin strip off
the back edge of the wings. Fold
the glider and trim both wings
together, so they are the same.
Trim the glider until it flies really
well.

### Balancing the glider

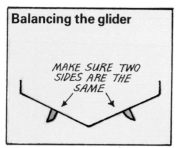

MAKE SURE TWO
SIDES ARE THE
SAME

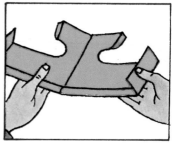

If it swerves, the glider may not
be properly balanced. Look at it
head on and push the wings up
or down to make them level.

If it still swerves, you may need
to bend one of the fins in further
than the other. Adjust the fins
until it flies straight.

30   * You can find out about elevators on pages 24–26.

# Fast launch

Here is a special launch which makes the glider go very fast. Hold the front edge between your finger and thumb, with your hand underneath the glider, as shown on the right. Then move your hand forward fast. Let go almost immediately and pull your hand out of the way.

If you launch the glider like this and throw it up steeply, it should loop the loop. It may take a bit of practice to do this.

## A flying competition

Can you invent some more glider designs? You could have a competition to see whose glider flies the furthest when launched from the same height, or whose glider is best at looping the loop.

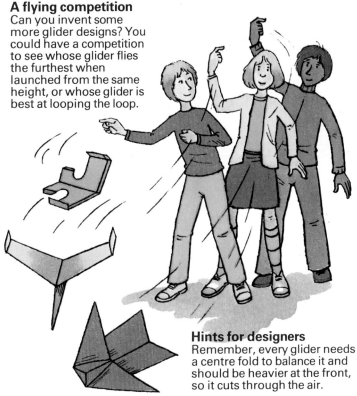

### Hints for designers

Remember, every glider needs a centre fold to balance it and should be heavier at the front, so it cuts through the air.

31

# Lifting things on air

On these two pages there are lots of tricks you can do, making things rise up and hover in the air. All these tricks are based on a scientific discovery made in 1738, by a Swiss scientist called Bernoulli. Bernoulli found that moving air has less pressure than the still air around it. This is called the Bernoulli principle.

**1 Paper strip trick**

Cut a strip of paper and hold one end against your chin, just below your bottom lip. Then blow straight ahead.

**2**

The paper should lift up and flutter about, as it is sucked into the air stream of your breath.

**3 Why it happens**

LOW PRESSURE

The moving air of your breath has less pressure than the still air below the paper.

**4**

AIR PUSHES UP

The still air pushes up into the low pressure area and lifts the paper up with it.

**How planes fly**

The Bernoulli principle also explains how planes can fly. You can find out about this over the page.

## Jumping coin trick

Put a saucer about 10cm from the edge of a table and lay a small coin or cardboard disk in front.

Rest your bottom lip against the table edge and blow across the top of the coin.

Air trapped under the coin has more pressure than the air you blow, and it lifts the coin up.

## 1 Hovering ping-pong ball

Put some plasticine on one end of a cotton reel, leaving the hole clear. Push four nails into the plasticine. Then put a wide drinking straw (or two narrow ones) into the hole at the other end. Balance the ping-pong ball on the nails and blow up through the straw. The ball hovers just above the reel.

## 3 How it hovers

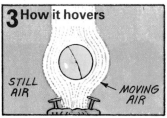

When you blow, your breath lifts the ball up and then flows round it. The air stream with the ball inside is held in position by the still air pushing in all round.

## Paper trick

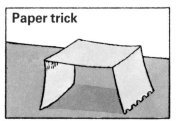

Can you think of a way to flatten this paper using the Bernoulli principle? The answer is on page 61.

33

# How aeroplanes fly

The Bernoulli principle*, which states that moving air has a lower pressure than the air around it, is one of the main reasons why planes can fly. Here is a model wing you can make, to see how the Bernoulli principle works.

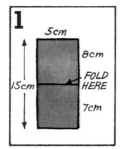

**1**

5cm
8cm
FOLD HERE
15cm
7cm

Take a piece of stiff paper 15cm×5cm. Fold the long side 8cm from the end.

**2** ROLL

Roll the longer part evenly round a thick pen or pencil to make it bulge.

**3** TAPE

Tape the ends together so the top of the model wing is curved and the bottom is flat as shown. This shape is called an aerofoil.

**4** TAILPLANE

An aeroplane's wings and tailplane have this special aerofoil shape. Helicopter rotors are shaped like this too.

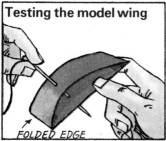

## Testing the model wing

FOLDED EDGE

Thread a piece of cotton about 40cm long through the aerofoil, about one third of the way back from the fold.

TILT COTTON SLIGHTLY

Hold the cotton tight between both hands and blow straight at the folded edge of the aerofoil. It should move up the cotton.

## How an aerofoil works

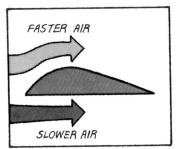

The air flowing over the curved top of the wing travels further and faster than the air below, so it has less pressure.

The higher pressure air below pushes the wing up. This is called "lift". It is the main force that keeps a plane in the air.

## How a plane takes off

Here are the forces which act on a plane as it takes off.

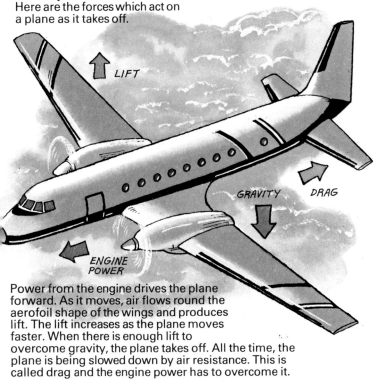

Power from the engine drives the plane forward. As it moves, air flows round the aerofoil shape of the wings and produces lift. The lift increases as the plane moves faster. When there is enough lift to overcome gravity, the plane takes off. All the time, the plane is being slowed down by air resistance. This is called drag and the engine power has to overcome it.

# Testing for floaters and sinkers

In this part of the book there are lots of experiments to do to find out how things float. For these you need a large bowl of water – a washing-up bowl or the sink or bath would do – and one or two jam jars.

First try testing things to see whether they float. The list below gives some ideas for things to test, but try anything you can find. Then make a chart of "floaters" and "sinkers".

### Ideas for things to test
Ping-pong ball
Marble
Rubber
Empty glass jar with its lid on
Piece of wood
Candle
Plasticine
Nail
Plastic counter
Pumice stone
Coin
Plastic pot (e.g. yogurt pot)
Needle

### Something to think about

Objects full of air, such as an airbed, or the glass jar with its lid on, are usually good floaters.

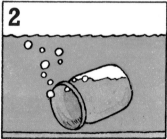

Try taking the lid off the jar and watch it sink as it fills with water. It seems that the air inside was keeping it afloat.

When you have tested everything examine your chart. Do the things which float have anything in common?

## A superfloater

See if you can find a polystyrene tray, like those in which meat is sold in supermarkets, and try floating it.

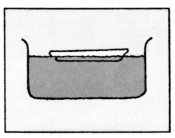

Why do you think it floats so well, hardly sinking into the water at all? It is not just because it is light – a needle is light too, but it sinks.

**3**

Solid objects though, such as candles and wood, float too. So there must be another reason why things float.

Try loading the tray with coins and watch it float lower and lower in the water. How much load can it carry before sinking?

# Making sinkers float

Some materials, such as wood, are natural floaters and some, such as plasticine, are sinkers. It is possible, though, to make sinkers float. You can find out how below.

Find a lump of plasticine about the size of a ping-pong ball and some marbles. Work the plasticine into a hollow bowl-shape, making sure there are no cracks in it.

Now try floating it. If it sinks, try making the sides higher and test it again. Keep adjusting the shape until it floats. Then see how many marbles it can carry.*

### Boat designing

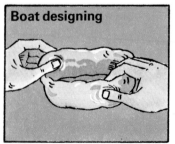

Can you redesign the plasticine boat to carry more marbles? Try making the bottom flatter and the sides higher and thinner.

### Competition

Give each person an equal amount of plasticine and see whose boat can carry the most marbles.

* You can find out why the bowl-shape floats over the page.

# Wooden boats and iron boats

BOWL-SHAPED HULL

BRUNEL'S SHIP THE "GREAT EASTERN"

At one time people thought boats could only be made from natural floaters, such as wood. They were amazed when engineers said they could make boats from iron which is a sinker. As with plasticine, iron has to be made into a hollow, bowl-shape in order to make it float.

Iron was better for ship-building than wood because it lasted longer and the ships could be made much bigger. In 1858 an engineer called Brunel built an iron ship 211m long, which at that time was far longer than any other ship in the world.

## Candle puzzle

If you float a candle in water like this, how far do you think it can burn down before going out? To find out, cut about 3cm from the top of a candle and push a nail into the bottom. Then try floating it. If it sinks use a lighter nail. If it floats on its side, you need a heavier nail. When it floats upright, light the wick and wait to see what happens. (Answer on page 61.)

WICK MAY TAKE A WHILE TO LIGHT IF IT IS WET

NAIL

39

# How things float

Here is an experiment which shows why a lump of plasticine sinks, but a plasticine bowl-shape floats. To do it, you need to find a large jar with a neck wide enough to fit your hand through.

Put some water in the jar and mark the level with a felt-tip pen. Then drop a lump of plasticine in and mark the level again. You could use a different coloured pen.

The level of the water rises because the ball pushes away, or "displaces" water to make room for itself.

Now make the ball of plasticine into a bowl-shape and float it on the water. Mark the level of the water again.

The level is even higher. This shows that the bowl displaces more water than the ball.

Now put your hand in a plastic bag and dip it in water. You can feel the displaced water pushing against it. A Greek scientist, Archimedes, discovered how this force of water can make things float.

## What Archimedes found out

Archimedes lived in Greece over 2,000 years ago. One day he filled his bath too full and when he got in, it overflowed. He did some experiments to find out how much water overflowed and worked out that the amount of water an object displaces is equal to the volume of the object.

Later he worked out that the strength of the force pushing back against an object depends on how much water it displaces. If an object displaces enough water to make a force strong enough to support its weight, then it floats.

## Why the bowl-shape floats

The plasticine bowl and ball weigh the same, but the bowl displaces more water because it is a larger shape. So there is a stronger force pushing against the bowl and this is why it can float.

If you put marbles in the bowl it has to displace more water in order to support the extra weight.

41

# Floating in salty water

Floating is easy in the Dead Sea, which lies between Israel and Jordan. People's bodies hardly sink into the water at all. This is because the water is so salty – seven times saltier than sea water usually is. Below you can find out how to make a special floater which measures how things float in ordinary water and in salty water (often called brine).

## Making brine

Pour a jar of warm water (not too hot) into a pan and add salt to it. Stir and keep adding salt until no more will dissolve and it sinks to the bottom.

Leave it for several hours until the liquid is no longer cloudy. If a crust forms, push it to the bottom. Then pour off the clear brine into a labelled jar.

## 1 Making a special floater

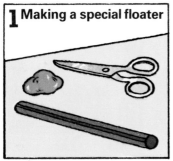

To test the brine, make a special floater from a plastic drinking straw and plasticine.

## 2

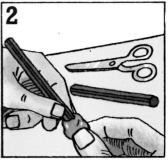

Cut a piece of straw about 6cm long and stick a small lump of plasticine on one end.

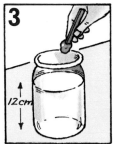

**3** Put it in a jar containing at least 12cm of water, to see how it floats.

LUMP TOO SMALL

**4** If it topples to one side, make the lump of plasticine bigger. Then test it again.

LUMP TOO BIG

**5** If it sinks to the bottom, the lump is too heavy so make it smaller.

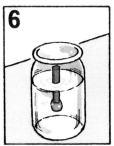

**6** Adjust it until it floats upright, with part of the straw above the water.

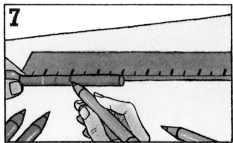

**7** Then take it out and dry the straw. Draw a scale on it by laying it alongside a ruler and making marks every 1cm with different coloured pens. Press hard to make clear marks.

**Testing water and brine**
Now you can use the floater to compare how things float in water and in brine. First see how deep the floater sinks into the water, by noting which mark on the scale the water level comes nearest to. Then see how deep it sinks into the brine. Over the page you can find out why the floater does not sink so far into the brine.

# Testing salty water

Things float better in brine than in water, because they do not have to sink so far into it. Here is a test to find out why. You can use the brine left from a previous experiment, or make some as described on page 42. You also need some water, a jam jar, a felt-tip pen and some kitchen scales.

Almost fill the jar with brine and mark the level it comes to. Then put the jar on the kitchen scales and note its weight.

Empty out the brine and fill the jar to the same level with water. Weigh the water. Is it heavier or lighter than the brine?

## Light and heavy liquids

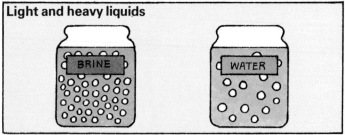

All substances are made up of particles. In brine the particles are closer together than they are in water, so there are more particles packed into the same space. Therefore if you have the same amount of brine as water, the brine is heavier. It is said to be denser than water.

44

The test on the opposite page shows that brine is heavier than water. Because of this, it pushes harder against objects floating in it than water does. So in order to float, things do not have to displace as much brine as they do water. This is why they do not sink so far into brine.

A special floater like the one described on the previous page, which measures how things float in different liquids, is called a hydrometer.

## How hydrometers are used

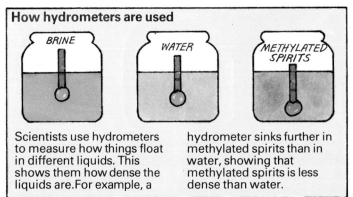

Scientists use hydrometers to measure how things float in different liquids. This shows them how dense the liquids are. For example, a hydrometer sinks further in methylated spirits than in water, showing that methylated spirits is less dense than water.

45

# Boatman puzzle

The theory of Archimedes (see page 41) may help you solve this puzzle, or you can try the test below.

A boatman loads his boat with iron bars and rows out into a small pond. Then he dumps the bars overboard. Does the water level in the pond rise, fall, or stay the same?

## Test to find the answer

Put some nails in a yogurt pot and float it in a large jar. Mark the water level.

Then tip the nails into the water and refloat the empty pot. What happens to the water level?*

  * Answer on page 61.

# Loading cargo

Ships which carry cargo have to be carefully designed so that the cargo does not slide about when the ship is in rough water. To see what could happen to a ship with "shifting" cargo, try making a paper boat as shown below, then float it and load it with marbles.

Can you think of a way to stop the marbles rolling to one end? The section below about tankers may give you an idea.

## How to make a paper boat

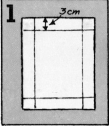

**1**
On a piece of paper, draw lines like this 3cm in from the edges. Fold along the lines.

**2**
Make two cuts at each corner along the lines shown here in red, to make tabs.

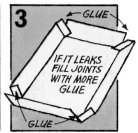

**3**
GLUE
IF IT LEAKS FILL JOINTS WITH MORE GLUE
GLUE

Bend the sides up and stick the tabs to the ends with waterproof glue.

## Tankers

Tankers are specially designed with very large holds for carrying oil and other chemicals.

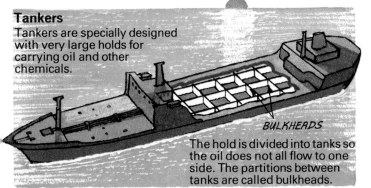

BULKHEADS

The hold is divided into tanks so the oil does not all flow to one side. The partitions between tanks are called bulkheads.

# Egg trick

If you put an egg in water, it sinks to the bottom. Can you work out how to make it float half-way up a jar, like the one shown here?

You can find out how to do it below. Then you could try the trick on your friends, to see if they can work it out.

Make some brine, as on page 42, by stirring salt into warm water. Leave it to settle for several hours, then pour off the clear brine.

Half fill a wide-necked jar, or glass jug, with brine and put a fresh egg into it. It should float, even if you push it under.

Tilt the jar and *very gently* pour water into it until it is full. Now the egg should be floating half-way up the jar.

POUR WATER
AGAINST
SIDE OF
JAR

## How it works

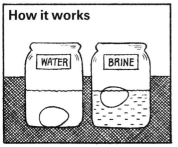
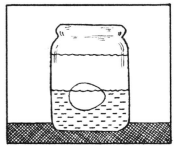

The egg floats in brine but not in water because brine is denser than water and can support the egg's weight.

Water, as it is less dense, also floats on brine. So in fact, both the egg and the water are floating on the brine.

## Test to prove it

Colour some water with a few drops of ink. Then gently pour it on to some brine in a jar, by

tilting the jar as you did before. Take care not to pour too hard, or the brine and water will mix.

## Did you know?

A ship floats at different levels depending on the weight of its cargo and the kind of water it is sailing through. It floats lower in fresh river water than in salty sea water, and also in warm water which is less dense than cold.

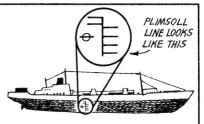

PLIMSOLL LINE LOOKS LIKE THIS

Every ship has a special mark on the side, to show how deeply the fully-loaded ship should float in different kinds of water.

The mark is called the Plimsoll Line, after Samuel Plimsoll. He introduced it in 1885, to protect sailors from shipowners who loaded so much cargo on to their ships that they were likely to sink.

# Special floaters

If you drop a needle in water, it sinks. It is so small it cannot push away enough water to support its weight. It is possible, though, to make a needle float right on top of the surface of the water. Can you work out how?

## How to do it
Put some water into a clean bowl or jar. Make sure the needle is dry, then rest it across a fork. Lower the needle gently on to the water and pull the fork out carefully.

## How it works

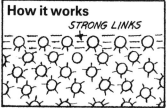

STRONG LINKS

Water, like everything else, is made up of tiny particles, called molecules. The molecules at the surface are more strongly linked than those below and act like a kind of skin. This is called surface tension.

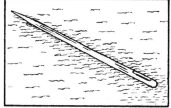

If you put the needle very gently on to the water, it rests on top of the surface. You can probably see that the surface is dented where the needle is lying.

## Walking on water
Have you ever seen an insect skating across the surface of a pond? Like the needle, it is supported by the surface tension of the water. You may see round hollows where the insect's feet press down the surface of the water.

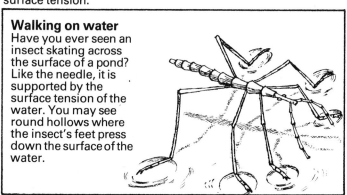

## A speedboat to make

To make this simple boat which speeds across the surface of the water, you need some thin card and washing-up liquid.

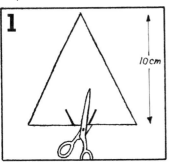

**1**

10cm

Cut a triangle of thin card, about 10cm long, and make two small cuts in the base as shown.

**2**

FLAP

Bend up the flap between the cuts and then float the boat in some clean, shallow water.

**3**

TOUCH HERE

Put a drop of washing-up liquid on your finger and touch the water in the gap at the back of the boat with it. The boat should shoot forward.

### How it works
Washing-up liquid stops the molecules at the surface clinging together and so decreases the surface tension of the water.

The boat is resting on the surface of the water and the drop of washing-up liquid at the back decreases the tension there. The boat is pulled forward by the stronger tension at the front. To do it again you need fresh water and a new boat.

# Pen-top diver

Here is how to make a pen-top dive like a submarine to the bottom of a bottle and come back up again. You need a plastic pen-top, some metal paper-clips, a candle and a plastic bottle with a screw-cap.

**1** STICK CANDLE TO SAUCER WITH WAX

Bend out one end of a paper-clip and heat it in a candle flame. Then use the hot wire to melt a hole in the pen-top as shown here.

**2** PUT CANDLE OUT →

Put the candle out. Then push a new paper-clip through the hole in the pen-top and hook another clip to it, to make a chain.

**3** BOTTLE FULL TO BRIM

Fill the bottle with water and drop the pen-top in. It should float with the tip just showing. If it sinks use a smaller paper-clip.

## How it works

When you put the diver in water, an air bubble is trapped inside it.

The bottle is full to the brim, so when you squeeze it, the water has nowhere to go. It pushes further into the diver and squashes the air bubble into a smaller space.

**4**

Now screw the cap on tightly and squeeze the bottle. The "diver" should go right down to the bottom of the bottle and come back up when you stop squeezing.

If it does not work, you may need to add another paper-clip to the pen-top so it does not float so well. Make sure, too, that the bottle is full to the brim.

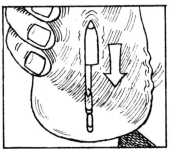

Now there is more water in the diver so it is heavier. This makes it too heavy to float, so it sinks to the bottom of the bottle.

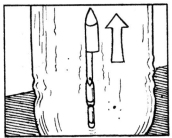

When you relax the pressure, the air bubble expands and pushes the extra water out of the diver, so it is lighter and comes up again.

53

# How a submarine works

A submarine can dive under water and come up to the surface again by altering its weight. To do this it has big tanks called ballast tanks, which can be filled and emptied. You can find out how they work below.

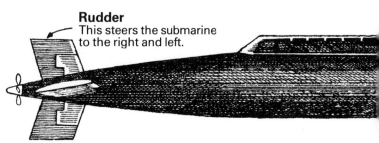

**Rudder**
This steers the submarine to the right and left.

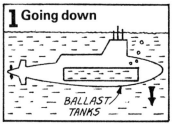

**1 Going down**

The ballast tanks are filled with water through flood holes in the bottom of the tanks and the air is forced out. This makes the submarine heavier, so it sinks.

*BALLAST TANKS*

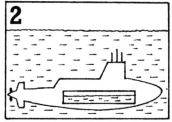

**2**

To stop the submarine sinking, air is pumped back into the tanks to push out some of the water and make the submarine lighter.

**3**

As the submarine uses up fuel and other supplies, it becomes lighter. To make up for this it has another set of tanks, called trim tanks, which are filled with water to replace the weight lost.

*TRIM TANKS*

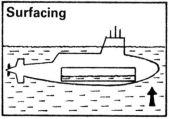

**Surfacing**

To make the submarine come up again, more air is pumped into the ballast tanks and most of the water is pushed out. This makes the submarine light enough to float, so it rises.

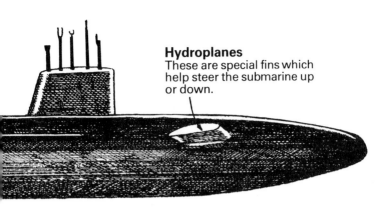

## Hydroplanes

These are special fins which help steer the submarine up or down.

## How hydroplanes work

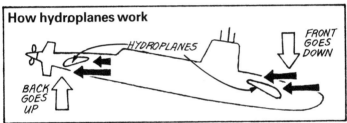

HYDROPLANES

FRONT GOES DOWN

BACK GOES UP

To dive, the back of the rear hydroplanes are dipped, so water pressing underneath them forces the back of the submarine up. The front hydroplanes are dipped so water pressing on top of them forces the front down.

## Why a hot air balloon is like a submarine

A hot air balloon is like a submarine floating in an ocean of air.

The balloon is filled with hot air, which is less dense and so lighter than the cooler air around it. This makes the balloon rise. When the air in the balloon cools, it gets heavier and sinks, just like a submarine with its ballast tanks full of water.

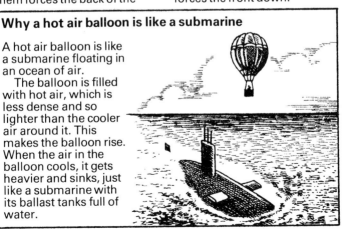

55

# Emergency floaters

Knowing the best way to float could help you in an emergency. For instance, a person afraid of drowning usually panics and waves his arms about. This only makes it more difficult to float, though. To find out why, try making a dummy body as shown below and testing it with its arms in different positions. You will need a metal tube with a cap, such as a cigar tube, a clothes peg, plasticine and a rubber band.

**1**

Put some plasticine in the tube, screw the cap on and try floating it. Add or take out plasticine until it floats with the top just level with the water.

**2**

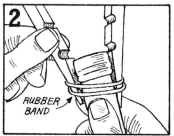

RUBBER BAND

To make "arms", wind a rubber band round the top of the tube, then pull a peg apart and push the bits of peg under the band, so they stick upwards.

**3**

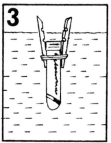

Float the dummy with its arms in this position. Its top goes underwater.

**4**

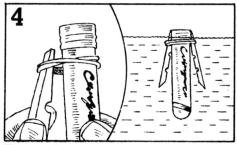

Then push the pegs in the other way. Now the arms are under the water and the dummy displaces more water, so it floats a little better. This also happens with a real body.

56

# Life-saver puzzle

Here is a puzzle to see how many life-savers you can spot.

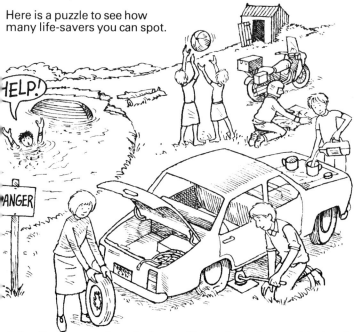

A family, out on a day-trip, has stopped by a lake to change a punctured wheel on the car. One of the children takes a boat out on to the lake, then leans over too far and topples in.

The water is deep and the boy is in danger of drowning, but nobody can swim. Look in the picture to see how many things there are which could be used to save him. (Answer on page 61.)

## Breathing and floating

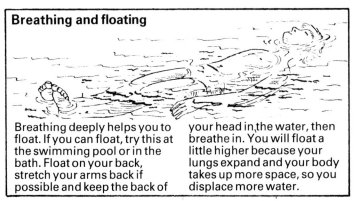

Breathing deeply helps you to float. If you can float, try this at the swimming pool or in the bath. Float on your back, stretch your arms back if possible and keep the back of your head in the water, then breathe in. You will float a little higher because your lungs expand and your body takes up more space, so you displace more water.

# Weight and weightlessness

Below there is an experiment you can do to show that falling things are weightless.

When you pick up a bag of potatoes, what you feel as weight is the force you are using to resist the pull of gravity on the bag. If you let the bag fall, it is no longer resisting the pull of gravity so it becomes weightless. In the same way, a parachutist who jumps from a plane and starts falling is weightless.

The parachutist is weightless until his parachute opens and resists the pull of gravity on him.

**1 Experiment**

Put a brick, or a heavy book, on a pair of bathroom scales and note the weight. Then hold them over a soft bed.

**2**

Watching the weight-reading all the time, drop the scales with the book on top, on to the bed. What happens to the weight?

**Explanation**

As the scales fall towards the bed, the reading swings right back below zero. The book has become weightless because it is falling and no longer resisting gravity.

As soon as everything hits the bed, gravity is being resisted again and the book weighs the same as before.

# How astronauts lose weight

Below you can find out why astronauts in a satellite float weightless in their cabin.

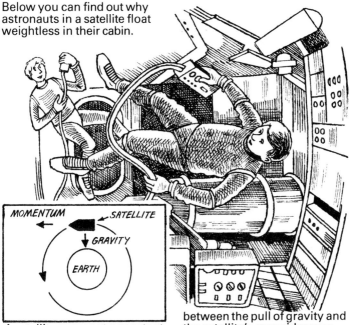

MOMENTUM — SATELLITE
GRAVITY
EARTH

A satellite moves at a constant speed because there is no air to slow it down. If there were no pull of gravity, the satellite would move sideways. However the satellite also falls under gravity. The balance between the pull of gravity and the satellite's own sideways movement keep it in orbit round the Earth. The satellite and astronauts are not resisting the pull of gravity. They are falling freely like the book and so are weightless.

## Lift puzzle

Imagine you are standing on some scales in a lift. What happens to the weight-reading as the lift goes down? The experiment on the opposite page may help you solve this puzzle.
The answer is on page 61.

GOING DOWN!

# Ice-cube puzzle

This ice-cube is floating in a glass full of water. What do you think will happen when the ice-cube melts? Will the glass overflow?

Before you look at the answer on the opposite page, try the experiment below – it may give you a clue.

## 1 Experiment

Put some water in a paper or plastic cup and mark the level with a felt-tip pen. Then put it in the freezer and leave it for several hours.

## 2

When it is frozen, check the level. It should be higher now, because water expands when it freezes. What happens to the level when the ice melts again?

### Icebergs

Only about one tenth of an iceberg shows above the sea. This is because when water freezes and changes to ice, it takes up about one tenth more space than it did as water.

The hidden part of icebergs can be very dangerous to ships, as they can be torn open by the jagged, underwater ice peaks.

# Puzzle answers

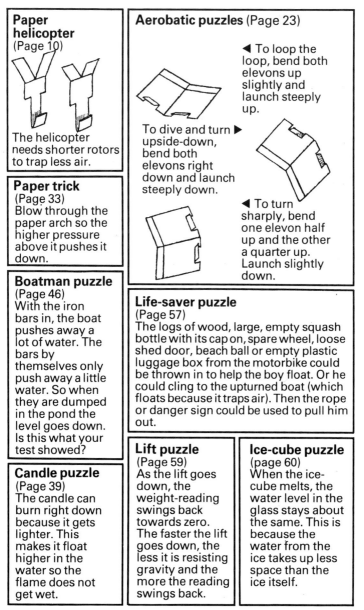

### Paper helicopter
(Page 10)

The helicopter needs shorter rotors to trap less air.

### Paper trick
(Page 33)
Blow through the paper arch so the higher pressure above it pushes it down.

### Boatman puzzle
(Page 46)
With the iron bars in, the boat pushes away a lot of water. The bars by themselves only push away a little water. So when they are dumped in the pond the level goes down. Is this what your test showed?

### Candle puzzle
(Page 39)
The candle can burn right down because it gets lighter. This makes it float higher in the water so the flame does not get wet.

### Aerobatic puzzles (Page 23)

◀ To loop the loop, bend both elevons up slightly and launch steeply up.

To dive and turn ▶ upside-down, bend both elevons right down and launch steeply down.

◀ To turn sharply, bend one elevon half up and the other a quarter up. Launch slightly down.

### Life-saver puzzle
(Page 57)
The logs of wood, large, empty squash bottle with its cap on, spare wheel, loose shed door, beach ball or empty plastic luggage box from the motorbike could be thrown in to help the boy float. Or he could cling to the upturned boat (which floats because it traps air). Then the rope or danger sign could be used to pull him out.

### Lift puzzle
(Page 59)
As the lift goes down, the weight-reading swings back towards zero. The faster the lift goes down, the less it is resisting gravity and the more the reading swings back.

### Ice-cube puzzle
(page 60)
When the ice-cube melts, the water level in the glass stays about the same. This is because the water from the ice takes up less space than the ice itself.

# Pattern for Mark 2 glider

Here is the pattern for the glider on page 24. Fold the paper you are using to make the glider as shown on page 24. Then trace all the lines of this pattern on to the paper, making sure that the bottom line is along the fold, as shown.

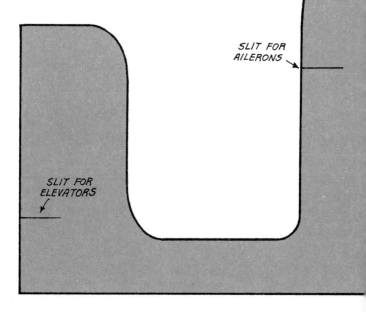

SLIT FOR AILERONS

SLIT FOR ELEVATORS

PLACE THIS LINE ALONG
FOLD IN PAPER

# Index

# CHEMISTRY
# EXPERIMENTS

# Chemistry experiments

This part of the book is full of simple experiments using equipment and chemicals that you can find at home. There are experiments to do to make a gas, split water and copperplate a key, and you can test fizzy drinks to see what makes them fizz. There are tests to do, too, on sweets and washing powders and you can make bath salts and invisible inks and find out how they work.

Over the page there are some hints on being a chemist, and a list of useful things to collect for your "lab". On pages 126-127, there are lists of all the equipment you need for each experiment.

Before you do any experiments read through the guidelines and safety hints on page 70-73. If you follow these carefully, your experiments will be more successful.

# Being a chemist

Everything around us is made up of chemicals. Chemistry is the study of chemicals and how they behave when you mix them and heat them, cool them or do other things to them. The ways the chemicals behave are called chemical reactions. Chemical reactions are happening all the time. For instance, when food is cooked, when a bicycle goes rusty and when coal burns, chemical reactions are taking place.

Chemists do experiments to study the way chemicals react and find out more about them. Often they can work out what will happen before they do an experiment because they know the special characteristics, or "properties" of the different chemicals. They do experiments to check their theories.

Through their work they can create new substances, such as plastics and man-made fibres, and discover chemical reactions which are useful in medicine and industry.

This book shows you how to do simple experiments with chemicals such as lemon juice, washing soda and salt.

From these experiments you can find out the properties of the chemicals and see how they react, just like a real chemist.

## Setting up your lab

For your lab you need a place with a table or bench where you can do the experiments, and some shelves or a cupboard where you can keep your chemicals and equipment. It is useful to be near a sink, too. You should not do the experiments near food. Always put your chemicals away when you have finished, and keep them out of reach of young children.

## Things to collect

Jam jars with lids
Bottles with tops
Sticky labels
A pen or pencil
Drinking straws
Roll of paper towels
An old, blunt knife
An old tablespoon
Plastic teaspoons
Ruler
Notepad
A cloth and an old toothbrush
  for cleaning equipment

OVERALL OR APRON TO PROTECT YOUR CLOTHES

NEWSPAPER TO COVER TABLE OR CARPET

Above is a list of the things you need in your lab. You can do most of the experiments in jars, but for a few, test-tubes are better. You can find out where to buy test-tubes, and other useful equipment, on page 125. There are some suggestions for equipment to make yourself on pages 120-123.

**1 Chemicals**

You will find most of the chemicals you need at home. Keep small amounts of them in labelled jars or bottles.

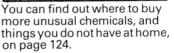

**2**

You can find out where to buy more unusual chemicals, and things you do not have at home, on page 124.

# Doing experiments

On the next few pages there are some hints and guidelines to help make your experiments successful. The experiments may not always work first time, though, and chemists sometimes have to repeat experiments several times. If one of your experiments does not work, read the instructions again and try to work out what went wrong. Here are some important points to remember.

**1** Read all the instructions for an experiment before you start, so you know what to do, and make sure you have everything you need.

**2** Make sure all your equipment is clean and dry. If it is wet or dirty, the experiment may not work.

**3** Measure the amounts of chemicals you use very carefully. You can find out how to do this over the page.

**4** Stick labels on all the jars and test-tubes you use, so you know what is in them.

**5** Always use clean, dry spoons for measuring and stirring different chemicals.

**6** Watch carefully to see what happens in the experiment. Note down any changes in colour, bubbles of gas or other reactions.

**7** If an experiment does not work, wash all the equipment and start again. If it keeps on going wrong, try using a completely different set of equipment.*

*There may be something on one of the jars or test-tubes which will not wash off.

## Cleaning your equipment

As soon as you finish an experiment,* wash all the equipment in warm, soapy water, rinse it well, and dry with a paper towel. If you do not wash your equipment straight away, it may be very difficult to get clean.

An old toothbrush is good for cleaning test-tubes and scrubbing ring-marks off jars.

### 1 Labelling

You should always label the jars or test-tubes you use for the chemicals in an experiment, even if there are only two of them. It is very easy to forget which is which during the experiment.

You can make labels from paper and sticky tape, or buy sticky labels from a stationery shop.

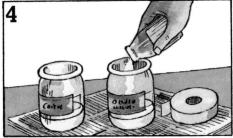

Write the labels in pencil or crayon so they do not smudge.

It is easier to write the labels before you stick them on the jars. To avoid spilling the chemicals, stick the labels on the jars before you put the chemicals in.

*Pour chemicals away down the sink or lavatory – see "Safety hints" on the next page.

## Measuring

It is very important to measure out chemicals carefully and accurately, and to use exactly the amounts given in the instructions. If you do not, the experiment may not work properly. When you are doing the same experiment on two different substances to compare them, make sure you use equal amounts of the substances, or the experiment will not be fair. Here are some ways to measure chemicals.

For lots of the experiments you can measure the chemicals in spoonfuls. A spoonful of dry substance should be rounded, not heaped.

To measure out equal amounts of liquids, use a jar. Mark a line anywhere on the jar with a felt-tip pen. To measure each liquid, fill the jar up to the line.

In some experiments the instructions tell you to measure the depth of the liquid in a jar. It does not matter how big your jar is.

### Dissolving

To dissolve a substance in a liquid you have to stir it for several minutes, then leave it for a while and stir again.

When a substance dissolves, it disappears and becomes part of the liquid. Some substances never dissolve completely though.

# Safety hints

All the experiments in this book are quite safe, and most of the chemicals are harmless. However, even harmless substances can be dangerous if you mix them wrongly, so always take great care and follow the instructions. Below there is a checklist of safety points to remember.

Never invent your own experiments, or play with chemicals. Always take care to follow instructions.

Label all chemicals clearly and keep them away from young children, on a high shelf or in a cupboard you can lock. You must be especially careful with chemicals such as copper sulphate, which is poisonous. Mark "HARMFUL" in big letters on the label.

Keep a set of equipment, such as knives and spoons, for use only in the experiments. Buy them specially if you cannot find old ones that are no longer used.

Never taste or eat chemicals and do not experiment near food. Try not to rub your eyes or bite your nails while doing experiments.

When you have finished an experiment, wash the chemicals away down the sink with plenty of water. If they are dangerous chemicals, flush them down the lavatory. Then wash your hands.

Some chemists wear goggles to prevent chemicals going in their eyes. If you do get something in your eye, or spill a chemical on your hands or clothes, wash it away with plenty of water.

If you ever do have an accident with chemicals, go to a doctor immediately and tell him or her the name of the chemical involved.

# Acids at home

"Acid" is the name for a group of chemicals which share certain characteristics. Lots of the substances in your kitchen cupboard are acids. Most acids are sour. You will find out about some of their other characteristics as you do the experiments on the next few pages.

To find out which things are acids, you can test them with a liquid called an "indicator".

## How to make an indicator

**1** You can make an indicator from red cabbage.* Chop up about a quarter of a cabbage.

SMALL PIECES

**2** Put the pieces in a saucepan and add some boiling water – just enough to cover the cabbage.

**3** Stir, then leave the pieces to soak for at least 15 minutes.

**4** FILTER

Now you need to separate the liquid from the cabbage. You can do this by filtering it, as shown on the opposite page.

KEEP IN FRIDGE

INDICATOR

**5** Keep the filtered liquid in a bottle with a lid and label it. You will be using this indicator in lots of the experiments.

74    *If you cannot get red cabbage you can use rose petals (not white or yellow) or blackberries.*

# How to filter

## 1

SOLID BITS

LIQUID

Filtering is a way of straining a liquid to remove all the bits from it. Filtering removes even very fine particles from a liquid.

## 2

FUNNEL

FOLD IN HALF

FOLD AGAIN

To make a filter you need a piece of kitchen paper towel and a funnel.* Fold the paper towel in half, then in half again, as shown.

## 3

Hold three corners of the paper together and pull the other corner out, like this. This makes a cone shape which fits in the funnel.

## 4

KEEP LEVEL OF LIQUID BELOW TOP OF FUNNEL

Put the funnel in a bottle and pour the liquid into the paper. The solid bits stay in the paper and the pure liquid drips through into the bottle.

## Acid test

Now prepare some indicator for the acid test. Pour a little indicator into several jars and stick labels on all of them.

CONTROL

On one of the labels, write "CONTROL". You can find out how to do the test on the next page.

*You can find out where to buy a funnel on page 125.

# Testing for acids

Now you can use the indicator, prepared on the previous page, to find out how many acids you have at home. Here is a list of ideas for things to test.

## Things to test
Lemon juice
Bicarbonate of soda
Baking powder
Vinegar
Cola drink
A boiled sweet
Washing-up liquid
Washing soda
Liquid floor cleaner
Orange juice
Sour milk
Indigestion tablets
Tea (without milk)
Milk of magnesia

## How to do the test
To each jar of indicator, add a few drops (or bits) of one of the substances. Do not add anything to the control jar, though. Write the name of the substance on the label on the jar.

*DARK LIQUIDS SUCH AS TEA WILL MAKE THE INDICATOR LOOK BROWN, SO ADD VERY LITTLE*

Now compare the colour of the liquid in each jar with the colour of the indicator in the "control" jar. If the liquid has turned pink, the substance tested is an acid.

If the liquid turns blue or green, the substance belongs to a different group of chemicals called "alkalis".* In some of the jars it may take an hour or two for the colour to change.

76   *Petal indicator goes yellow and blackberry indicator goes blue or green.

## More about acids and alkalis

Acids and alkalis are two different groups of chemicals. Most acids are sour, like lemon juice and vinegar. Strong acids, such as sulphuric acid are corrosive, that is, they eat away other materials. Some alkalis are also corrosive and can be just as dangerous as acids.

Did you know that the poison in a bee sting is an acid and the poison in a wasp sting is an alkali?

**3**

LEMON =
BICARB OF SODA =
BAKING POWDER =
VINEGAR =

It is a good idea to write down which substances are acids and which are alkalis. Did you find any substances which were neither acid nor alkali?

## Using a control

CONTROL

A control is a copy of the experiment, on which you do not do the tests. Chemists use a control so they can be sure the results are due to the test itself, and not to the equipment.

# Making acids disappear

Here is an experiment to see what happens when you mix an acid and an alkali. For the acid you can use the juice of a lemon and for the alkali, some bicarbonate of soda. You need some red cabbage or blackberry indicator.*

Squeeze the lemon and put the juice in a jar labelled "ACID". Put about 2cm of water in another jar and stir in two teaspoons of bicarbonate of soda. Label this jar "ALKALI".

Now pour a little of the alkali into a clean jar and test it with indicator. It should go green or blue. Keep this as a control.

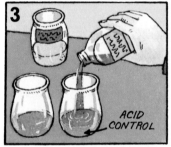

Pour some of the acid into two more jars. Add some indicator to both until they go pink. Put one jar on one side as a control.

Take the other jar of acid plus indicator and add a few drops of alkali to it, drop by drop. You could use an eyedropper.

As you add the alkali, the pink coloured liquid turns purple. This shows that the liquid is no longer an acid.

*Rose petal indicator does not work for this experiment.

## Where the acid goes

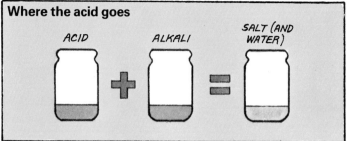

ACID + ALKALI = SALT (AND WATER)

When you mix an acid and an alkali, they make a different kind of chemical, called a "salt". Most salts are neutral, that is, neither acidic nor alkaline. This is why the liquid changed back to the same colour as the indicator.

### If it did not work

If your liquid went green, you added too much alkali. Try adding more acid to cancel out the extra alkali.

### Neutralizing stomach aches

Indigestion can be caused by too much acid in the stomach. Indigestion pills and powders are alkaline, so they cancel out the acid.

### More about salts

There are hundreds of different kinds of salts, including the salt we eat. This is called sodium chloride, and it is the result of the reaction between the alkali, sodium hydroxide and hydrochloric acid. These chemicals are very dangerous, but when they are mixed, they are neutralized and form a harmless salt.

79

# Water tests

Tap water is not pure – it has lots of chemicals from the rocks in the ground dissolved in it. Here is a test to find out how these chemicals affect the water.

For the test you need some distilled water which has had all the chemicals taken out of it. Distilled water is used in car batteries, so you may have some at home, or you can buy it from a garage or chemist.

EYEDROPPER

SOAP

You also need three jars with lids, an eyedropper* and some soap flakes, made by grating a bar of soap.

In one of the jars, make some soap solution by dissolving a tablespoonful of soap flakes in six tablespoons of hot water.

Put some tap water in one jar and the same amount of distilled water in another jar. Label the jars.

To make sure you have equal amounts put a line on a third jar and use that to measure out the distilled and tap water.

80  *You can find out where to buy an eyedropper on page 125.

## Doing the test

With the eyedropper, add five drops of soap solution to the jar of distilled water.

Put the lid on and shake the jar to see if the soap lathers. If it does not, add five more drops of soap and shake it again. Go on adding soap until it lathers and note how many drops it takes.

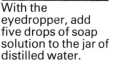

Now do the same test on the jar of tap water. Count how many drops of soap it needs to make a lather. If it needs a lot, add the drops 10 or 20 at a time.

Which water needed the most soap to lather? Water which needs a lot of soap is said to be "hard". If it lathers with very little soap, it is said to be "soft".

### What makes water hard

In the test, the tap water should need more soap than the distilled water, because the chemicals in tap water make it difficult for soap to lather.

The chemicals in tap water are calcium salts. When you add soap the calcium part of the salts reacts with the soap and makes scum. The soap will not lather until all the calcium in the water is used up. Over the page you can find out how to make hard water soft.

SCUM

## Making hard water soft

The tap water in some parts of the country is much harder than in others. This is because it has flowed over rocks which contain calcium salts. Here is an experiment to make hard water soft. You need tap water, washing soda and soap solution from the previous experiment.

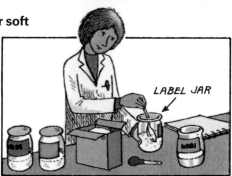

LABEL JAR

Measure the same amount of tap water as you used in the last experiment into a jar. Add a teaspoonful of washing soda and stir until it has all dissolved.

WASHING SODA

SOAP

When the washing soda has dissolved, add some drops of soap.* Shake the jar as before and see how many drops it needs to make a lather.

TAP WATER + WASHING SODA NEEDS ___

You should find that the water needs much less soap to make a lather than in the previous experiment. The washing soda has made the hardness disappear.

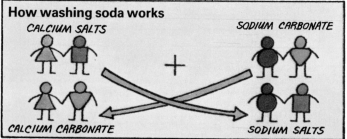

### How washing soda works

CALCIUM SALTS

SODIUM CARBONATE

CALCIUM CARBONATE

SODIUM SALTS

The chemical name for washing soda is sodium carbonate. The carbonate part of the washing soda joins up with the calcium in hard water and makes a new substance called calcium carbonate. The calcium is no longer able to react with the soap, so the soap can lather more easily.

82   *If your soap solution solidifies, add more hot water.

## Another water test

Now put some boiled tap water (the same amount as in previous tests) in a jar and let it cool. Add drops of soap.

Shake the jar and add more drops until the soap lathers. Does the boiled water need less soap than unboiled tap water?

## What boiling does

If the boiled water needed less soap to lather, the water is temporary hard water.* This has a calcium salt in it called calcium hydrogen carbonate. When the water boils, this calcium salt splits into calcium carbonate and carbon dioxide gas. The calcium carbonate sinks to the bottom and does not stop the soap lathering.

Calcium carbonate forms the substance in the kettle known as "fur". The carbon dioxide escapes in the steam.

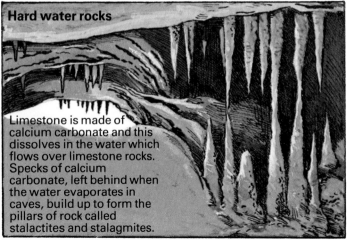

### Hard water rocks

Limestone is made of calcium carbonate and this dissolves in the water which flows over limestone rocks. Specks of calcium carbonate, left behind when the water evaporates in caves, build up to form the pillars of rock called stalactites and stalagmites.

*If boiling makes no difference to hard water, it is permanent hard water.

# How to make bath salts

Bath salts make bath water soft and soapy, and stop the soap making a scum. The water tests in the last few experiments showed how washing soda makes water soft, and you can use washing soda to make bath salts.

As well as washing soda, you need some food colouring, some cologne or perfume, a polythene bag, a rolling pin, a bowl and a jar to keep the bath salts in.

Put five tablespoons of washing soda in a polythene bag. Use the clear lumps of washing soda, not the powdery white ones near the top of the packet.

Break the lumps of washing soda into small pieces by rolling on the bag with the rolling pin.

STIR WITH YOUR HAND

Empty the washing soda into a bowl and add four or five drops of cologne or perfume, and some drops of food colouring.

**Experiment**
See what happens if you put some bath salts on a saucer and leave them in the air for a few days.

The bath salts go white and powdery, like the lumps of washing soda near the top of the packet. The crystals of washing soda contain water which escapes into the air, leaving the crystals white and powdery. So you should always keep the lid on your bath salts.

**4**

WASH BOWL AFTERWARDS

BATH SALTS

Stir in food colouring until all the washing soda is brightly coloured. Then tip it into a jar, screw on the lid and label it.

**5**

BATH SALTS

You could make several lots of bath salts using different food colourings, then mix them, or put them in layers in a jar.

# Soap tests

On this page you can find out how soap works, then, opposite, you can do a test to see which make of washing powder works the best. Some washing powders are called detergents. They are not made from the same substances as soap, but they work in the same way.

For the tests you will need several different makes of washing powder,* a piece of rag, some butter or margarine, several jars and some kitchen scales.

Smear a thick lump of butter on a small piece of rag. Put the rag in a jar and add a teaspoonful of washing powder. Then gently pour in some warm water and watch what happens.

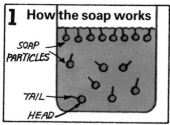

**1 How the soap works**

SOAP PARTICLES

TAIL

HEAD

Each tiny particle of soap has a head end and a tail end. The head loves water and the tail hates water.

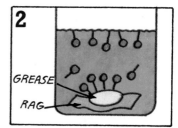

**2**

GREASE

RAG

The water-hating tails of the soap bury themselves in the grease and the water-loving heads stay in the water.

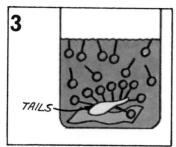

**3**

TAILS

More and more tails try to get into the grease, and they work their way between the grease and the cloth.

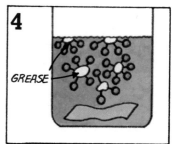

**4**

GREASE

They force the grease off the cloth and break it up into tiny balls. You could probably see this happening in the soap test.

*You could see if your neighbours have different kinds and will let

## Which powder works best?

Most washing powder manufacturers claim that their brand of powder washes whiter and cleaner than all the others. Here is a scientific way to test the powders.

For this test you need several different kinds of washing powder, some kitchen scales and a very dirty, greasy piece of rag. You could make the rag greasy by wiping it on a bicycle chain.

**1** Weigh out 25g of each powder and put each one in a separate labelled jar.

**2** Add the same amount of hot water to each jar to dissolve the powders.

**3** Put a small piece of greasy rag into each jar. Stir each 15 times and leave to soak overnight.

**4** Rinse each rag separately and put it back near its jar. Be careful not to mix them up.

**5** Now examine the pieces of rag and see which is the cleanest. You could make a chart showing which powders worked best, and how much they cost for 25g (divide packet price by total number of grammes, then multiply by 25).

*you have a small amount.*

**Another test**
Try testing each powder (dissolved in hot water) with red cabbage indicator to see if it is acid or alkaline.
Alkaline powders are not good for woollen fabrics and acid powders can be harmful to nylon.

# Soap powder eats egg experiment

For this experiment you will need some "biological" washing powder. This kind of powder has a special chemical in it which removes dirt by "eating" it. You can find out how in the experiment. You will also need some ordinary washing powder and an egg. To check if a powder is "biological", look on the packet for the words "acts biologically" or "digests dirt".

*THIS EXPERIMENT TAKES TWO DAYS*

Boil the egg for 10 minutes, so it is hard-boiled. Let it cool, then peel it.

Put a tablespoonful of each powder into two separate jars and label them.

*STIR*

Then put about 125ml (or eight tablespoons) warm water into each jar.

Cut two pieces of egg white, both the same size, and put them in the jars. Put the jars somewhere warm (near a radiator or in an airing cupboard) and leave them for two days.

## Two days later

Take the pieces of egg out of the jars and examine them. You should find that the egg from the biological powder is now smaller than the piece from the ordinary powder.

## How it works

EGG

ENZYME

The special chemical in the biological powder is called an "enzyme". The enzyme attacks the particles of egg and breaks them into smaller particles which dissolve in water. The egg in the other powder shows that egg does not dissolve in ordinary soapy water, and that it is the enzyme which "eats" the egg away.

**5**

If you cannot find somewhere warm, wrap the jars and put near a hot pipe.

## Enzymes in your stomach

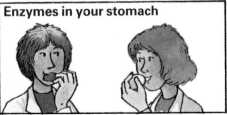

In your stomach you have lots of enzymes attacking the food you eat and breaking it up, just like the washing powder enzyme. The enzymes in your stomach break the food into molecules which can dissolve in your blood.

# Food tests

Our bodies need lots of different substances to keep them healthy, and we get these substances from the food we eat. One of these substances is called starch.

Here is a test to find out which foods contain starch. You need an eyedropper, a jar, newspaper and a chemical called iodine* which changes colour when you mix it with starch.

COVER TABLE WITH NEWSPAPER

EYEDROPPER

Pour a little iodine into the jar, then add the same amount of water to dilute it. Iodine stains, so be careful not to spill it.

## Doing the test

Now you can use the iodine to see which foods contain starch. Below there is a list of ideas for things to test.

THROW THE FOODS YOU TESTED AWAY WHEN YOU HAVE FINISHED

THINGS TO TEST

POTATO
APPLE
SALT
FLOUR
BUTTER
RICE
CHEESE
MEAT

CUT THE POTATO AND APPLE AND TEST THE INSIDE

Put a small piece of each type of food on the newspaper. Then, with the eyedropper, put a drop of iodine on to each of them and watch what happens.

If the iodine turns blue-black, or dark brown, it means the food contains starch. Note which foods contain starch. Do they have anything in common?

90    *You can buy this from a chemist. Ask for red tincture of iodine.

## Which foods contain starch

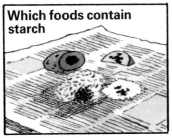

In the test, you probably found that only things which come from plants contain starch.

Starch is a substance made by plants, and we get the starch we need by eating food made from plants.

**1 Spit test**

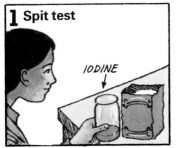

IODINE

This is a test to show what happens to starch when we eat it. You need some flour, iodine solution and a large mug.

**2**

Put a teaspoon of flour in a mug, add a little water and stir to make a paste. Then fill the mug with boiling water and stir.

**3**

Let it cool, then put a teaspoonful of the flour solution in a test-tube.

**4**

Pour one drop of the solution from the test-tube into a saucer or jar lid.

**5**

STAND TUBE IN A JAR

Then test the drop of solution with iodine to see if it contains starch.

Turn over ▶ 91

**6**

Now spit several times into the test-tube. Cover the top of the tube and shake it to mix the flour solution and spit.

**7**

WASH LID AFTER EACH TEST

Put the test-tube in a warm place. Every 20 minutes, pour out one drop, test it with iodine and see what colour the iodine goes.

### What happens

After several hours you should find that the iodine no longer changes colour, or only changes very slightly.

This shows that there is very little starch left in the solution. It has been "eaten" by the spit. You can find out how below.

### What spit does

The proper name for spit is saliva, and it contains an enzyme, like the washing powder on page 88-89.* Starch molecules are too big to be absorbed by our bodies and the enzyme in saliva breaks them up into the smaller molecules of a different substance called maltose.

In the spit test, the starch in the flour was changed to maltose, and this is why the iodine no longer changed colour.

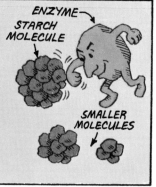

ENZYME

STARCH MOLECULE

SMALLER MOLECULES

*It is not the same enzyme as in the washing powder.

# More starch tests

Try testing white paper, paper glue and laundry starch (dissolved in hot water) with iodine, and see what happens.

The iodine should turn blue-black or brown, showing that these things contain starch. The starch is extracted from plants and treated to make a gluey substance which is used in paper glue and in laundry starch, and for making paper.

## Papermaking

A film of starch solution is often put on paper to hold the fibres of the paper together and give it a smooth surface.

## Laundry starch

In the same way, laundry starch forms a thin film on a fabric and helps to stiffen it and give it a smooth surface.

## Make your own glue

If you need some glue, but have run out, you can make some from flour and water. This glue is very good for sticking paper. People used to make wallpaper paste like this, but it tended to stain the paper and sometimes went mouldy.

To make the glue, mix a tablespoon of flour with a few drops of cold water to make a paste. Then stir in eight tablespoons of boiling water.

STIR WELL

Do not keep the glue too long, or it will go mouldy.

# What is gas?

Gas is the name for a group of airlike chemicals. There are lots of different kinds of gases. Most of them are invisible, but some gases have a smell. For instance, the gas hydrogen sulphide smells of bad eggs and is sometimes used to make stink bombs. Never sniff a gas though, as some are deadly poisonous.

On the next few pages you can make a gas and test it to find out what it is.

Air is a mixture of gases. The main ones are oxygen, which our bodies need to stay alive, and nitrogen.

You can sometimes see gas as bubbles in a liquid. The bubbles in a goldfish bowl are made by the gas the fish breathe out.

The bubbles in fizzy drinks are also a gas and the drink goes flat as the gas escapes.

THE GAS FROM STOVES AND GAS FIRES IS VERY DANGEROUS. IT CAN CAUSE EXPLOSIONS SO NEVER EXPERIMENT OR PLAY WITH IT!

Some gases burn well and are used for cooking and heating. One of these, called methane, occurs naturally in rocks underground and is also known as natural gas. Other kinds of gas for cooking and heating are manufactured from coal or oil.

# Making a gas

You can make a gas from washing soda and vinegar, as shown on the right. Try this, then make the equipment to catch the gas, so you can test it to find out what it is. The gas test is on the next page.

You need some washing soda and vinegar, a test-tube, plastic tubing,* plasticine and a liquid called limewater. You can buy limewater from some chemists or make it as shown on page 123.

To make the gas, pour 2cm vinegar into a small jar and add four or five lumps of washing soda. The mixture bubbles and fizzes as the gas escapes from it.

**1 Gas-catching equipment**

DO NOT BLOCK HOLE

Cut a piece of plastic tubing about 40cm long and wrap plasticine round one end.

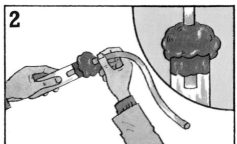

**2**

Push the end with the plasticine into the test-tube. It should fit tightly like a cork. If it is loose, take it out and add more plasticine.

**3**

BUNG

Now prepare the equipment for the test on the next page. Pull the bung out of the test-tube and have some vinegar and washing soda ready.

**4**

LIMEWATER

Pour a small amount of limewater into a clean jar or test-tube. The limewater should be about 0.5cm deep.

*See page 125 for where to buy plastic tubing and page 122 for another way to make gas-catching equipment.

## Testing the gas

Now you can test the gas made from washing soda and vinegar using the equipment shown on the previous page. You have to do the test quickly or the gas escapes, so read the instructions right through before you start.

Fill the test-tube one third full with vinegar and add four or five lumps of washing soda.

Then, as fast as you can, push the plasticine bung in the test-tube and hold the free end of the tubing in the limewater.

The gas should bubble out of the tube in the limewater. If nothing happens the bung may be leaking. Add more plasticine.

The mixture should go on making gas for about two minutes. Look carefully at the limewater. As the gas bubbles through it, the limewater should go cloudy.

## What the test shows

Limewater goes cloudy when the gas carbon dioxide is bubbled through it. So the gas made by mixing vinegar and washing soda must be carbon dioxide. You can find out what happens in this chemical reaction on the next page.

LIMEWATER

If your limewater did not go cloudy, try shaking it. If it still does not work, test the limewater as shown on page 123, to make sure it is the right kind.

KEEP END OF TUBE IN LIME-WATER

## Another gas to test

BE CAREFUL NOT TO SUCK LIMEWATER INTO YOUR MOUTH

You can try the limewater test on your breath. Dip one end of a drinking straw into some fresh limewater. Blow through it for two or three minutes and watch what happens to the limewater. What does this tell you about your breath?

# More gas-making experiments

Here are some more things you can mix to make a gas. Take anything from list A and mix it with something from list B. Each time, bubble the gas through limewater, as shown on the previous page, to see if it is carbon dioxide.

**A**
Vinegar
Juice of one lemon
Juice of half a
  grapefruit
Cola drink (left to
  settle for ten
  minutes)
Sour milk

**B**
Bicarbonate of soda
Limestone or chalk
  from the ground
  (not blackboard
  chalk)
An eggshell (broken
  into small pieces)
Washing soda

## How the gas is made

EGGSHELL
(= CALCIUM
CARBONATE)
+
VINEGAR
(=ETHANOIC
ACID)
GIVES
CARBON
DIOXIDE

Whatever you mix from lists A and B the limewater should turn cloudy. This is because all the things in list A are acids and all the things in list B are substances called carbonates. When you mix an acid with a carbonate, they react and make carbon dioxide.

For example, eggshell is made mainly of calcium carbonate, and vinegar is ethanoic acid. All carbonates contain carbon and oxygen. When you mix a carbonate with an acid, the carbon and oxygen escape as carbon dioxide gas.

## More about carbon dioxide

Carbon dioxide is one of the gases in air and, as the test on the previous page shows, when we breathe out, our breath contains carbon dioxide. There is only a tiny amount of carbon dioxide in the air though (about 0.03%).

Plants absorb carbon dioxide through their leaves and use it to make food. Plants give off oxygen, so they help to keep a good supply of oxygen in the air, and they use up carbon dioxide.

### Dry ice

Carbon dioxide can be made into a solid substance called "dry ice" which is much colder than ordinary ice. It is used in frozen food factories.

Smoke in plays is usually made from dry ice. When dry ice is plunged into boiling water the carbon dioxide evaporates and makes a white mist.

### Fire extinguishers

Carbon dioxide is good for fire-fighting and many fire-extinguishers contain compressed carbon dioxide. Things need oxygen to burn and when carbon dioxide is sprayed on a fire it pushes away the oxygen and so suffocates the flames.

# Making fizzy drinks

TESTING THE GAS

The bubbles of gas in fizzy drinks are carbon dioxide. You can check this by fitting gas-catching equipment to a bottle of fizzy drink and testing the gas with limewater, as shown on page 96.

You can make still drinks fizzy with a special powder made from bicarbonate of soda, citric acid crystals and icing sugar. Follow the instructions given below and use kitchen, not chemistry, utensils.

**1**

Put six teaspoons of citric acid crystals and three teaspoons of bicarbonate of soda into a bowl.

**2**

Then, with the back of the spoon, grind the two substances against the side of the bowl to make a fine powder.

**3**

Stir in two tablespoons of icing sugar. Then pour the mixture into a clean, dry jar with a screw-cap. Label it "FIZZ POWDER".

**4**

To make a fizzy drink, put two teaspoons of powder in a glass and fill it up with a still drink, such as orange or lime-juice.*

*If the drink tastes sour add more sugar to your powder.

# How it works

In the drink, the citric acid crystals dissolve and make citric acid. This reacts with the carbonate in bicarbonate of soda and makes carbon dioxide gas. The gas bubbles through the drink and makes it fizz.

When the reaction is over there is no more carbon dioxide and the drink goes flat. The sugar takes away the sour taste of the citric acid and bicarbonate of soda.

## How to make sherbet

You can use the same ingredients to make sherbet powder. Grind six teaspoons of citric acid crystals and three of bicarbonate of soda together as before, then stir in four tablespoons of icing sugar. Keep the sherbet powder in a jar with a screw-on lid.

When you lick the sherbet, the citric acid crystals dissolve and react with the bicarbonate of soda to make carbon dioxide gas. The fizz you feel on your tongue is the bubbles of gas.

# Chemical muddle puzzle

You can solve this puzzle by doing chemical tests. You need some flour, salt, icing sugar, cream of tartar, and bicarbonate of soda.

Chef Zabor is in a muddle. He has put his baking ingredients, flour, icing sugar, bicarbonate of soda, cream of tartar and salt, into jars and forgotten to label them. Now he needs a chemist to help sort out which is which.

## How to sort them out

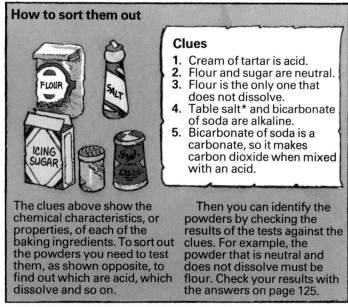

### Clues

1. Cream of tartar is acid.
2. Flour and sugar are neutral.
3. Flour is the only one that does not dissolve.
4. Table salt* and bicarbonate of soda are alkaline.
5. Bicarbonate of soda is a carbonate, so it makes carbon dioxide when mixed with an acid.

The clues above show the chemical characteristics, or properties, of each of the baking ingredients. To sort out the powders you need to test them, as shown opposite, to find out which are acid, which dissolve and so on.

Then you can identify the powders by checking the results of the tests against the clues. For example, the powder that is neutral and does not dissolve must be flour. Check your results with the answers on page 125.

*Salt is really neutral, but table salt contains a substance which makes it alkaline.

## Tests

**1.** Find out whether the powders are acid, alkaline or neutral, by doing the indicator test described on page 76.

**2.** Add warm water to each powder, stir and leave for a few minutes to see if it dissolves.

**3.** Mix each of the powders with an acid, such as vinegar, and do the gas test on page 96 to see if it makes carbon dioxide.

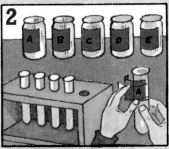

### 1 Doing the tests

CLEAN SPOON FOR EACH POWDER

Ask someone to put two teaspoons* of each ingredient into unlabelled jars, while you are not looking.

### 2

Label the jars A, B, C, D, E. Then label five test-tubes (or five more jars) A-E. Always test powder A in tube or jar A.

### 3

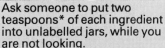

Use only a little of each powder in each test.* Wash the test-tubes out between tests.

### 4

| | A | B | C | D | E |
|---|---|---|---|---|---|
| INDICATOR TEST | ACID | | | | |
| WATER TEST | DISSOLVED | | | | |

Make a chart and fill in the results of each test. When you have done all the tests you will know the chemical properties of each powder. To identify them, match the properties with the clues given opposite.

*Use a clean teaspoon for each powder.

# Testing inks and dyes

Inks and dyes are made from coloured chemicals. To make all the different colours, lots of different coloured chemicals are mixed together, like mixing paints.

Here are some tests to separate the chemicals in felt-tip pens and sweets, so you can see all the different colours.

## Ink blob test

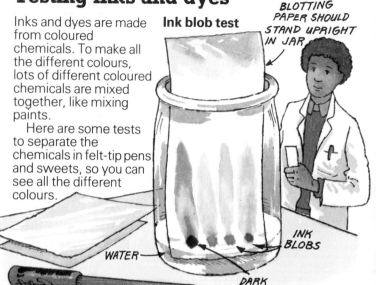

BLOTTING PAPER SHOULD STAND UPRIGHT IN JAR

WATER

INK BLOBS

DARK COLOURS WORK BEST

For this test you need some blotting paper, felt-tip pens and a jar with about 2cm of water in. Cut the blotting paper to make a strip just wide enough to fit in the jar. Then, about 5cm from one end, make blobs of colour with the felt-tip pens.

Put the paper in the jar, with the ink blobs at the bottom, and watch for about five minutes to see what happens. As the paper soaks up water, the blobs of ink separate into the different coloured chemicals of which they are made.

## How it works

As the water rises up the blotting paper it dissolves the chemicals and carries them up with it. Some chemicals are more easily absorbed by the blotting paper than others, so they travel up it at different speeds. As the different chemicals separate, you can see the different colours. Some colours, such as red and yellow, are made from only one chemical, so they do not separate.

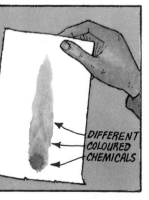

DIFFERENT COLOURED CHEMICALS

## Testing food colours

You can do the same test on coloured, sugar-coated sweets (such as "Smarties") to see how many different chemicals are used to colour them. The black or brown sweets work best.

Put three sweets, all the same colour, on a saucer and add three or four drops of water.

Turn the sweets over and over so all the colour runs off into the water.

Cut a long, thin strip of blotting paper and dip one end into the coloured water.

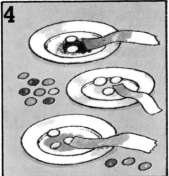

Leave the blotting paper in the water for about five minutes and watch what happens. Then try the test with different coloured sweets.

### How it works

The coloured chemicals from the sweets are absorbed by the blotting paper in the same way as the chemicals in the inks. As they are absorbed at different rates, the chemicals separate and you can see the different colours.

Separating chemicals like this, by absorbing them, is called "chromatography". Over the page there is another chromatography experiment.

# Detecting forgeries

The crook in the picture on the right is tampering with the figures on a cheque. He is changing the sum from 60 to 60,000 by adding noughts. You could prove the noughts were forged with a different pen, by doing a chromatography test.*

Here is an experiment to show how the test would work. You need two, different, black felt-tip pens, blotting paper and a jar with about 2cm of water in.

**1** Cut a piece of blotting paper just wide enough to fit in the jar.

**2** About 5cm from the bottom of the paper, write the figure 60 with one of the pens.

**3** With the other pen, add three noughts to the figure to make 60,000.

**4** Now put the blotting paper in the jar and watch what happens.

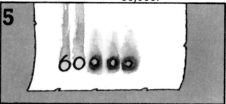

**5** The inks from the two pens separate into the different coloured chemicals of which they are made. Different manufacturers use different chemicals in their inks, so the pattern of colours from the two pens is not the same and you can see that the noughts were added with a different pen.

*You can find out about chromatography on the previous page.

# Invisible ink experiments

Invisible inks are made from colourless chemicals which, when you burn them, or treat them with other chemicals, react and become coloured.

Here and on the next two pages there are two different ways of making invisible ink. The lemon juice ink on this page is easier than the one in the next experiment, so try this one first.

**1 Lemon juice ink**

For this ink you need the juice of a lemon, a piece of paper and a thin paintbrush to write with.

**2** LEMON JUICE

Write a message with the lemon juice, dipping the brush in the juice between each letter. Leave to dry for at least an hour, or until the writing is invisible.

**3** TOP SHELF

To reveal the message put the paper, face down, on a shelf in the oven. Set the oven at 175°C (350°F), or gas mark 4, and leave for ten minutes.

**4**

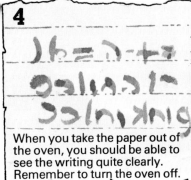

When you take the paper out of the oven, you should be able to see the writing quite clearly. Remember to turn the oven off.

## How it works

The lemon juice burns in the heat of the oven, but the oven is not hot enough to burn the paper. Burning is a chemical reaction which changes the lemon juice and makes it go brown. So the letters of the message appear as brown marks of burnt lemon juice.

## Another invisible ink

Here is another way to make invisible ink, using a special chemical which turns pink when you "develop" it with washing soda solution. It is quite difficult to do this and the ink may not work first time, so keep trying.

The chemical for the ink is called phenolphthalein.* This is used in some makes of laxative pills which you can buy from a chemist. Check on the packet that the pills do contain this chemical. You also need some washing soda and a paintbrush.

You need to use five or six of the pills. If they have a coloured coating, scrape it off with a knife.

CRUSH PILLS

Put the pills in a jar and crush them to a fine powder with the back of a spoon.

Fill the jar about 3cm deep with warm water and stir to dissolve the powder.

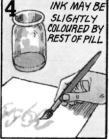

INK MAY BE SLIGHTLY COLOURED BY REST OF PILL

Write a message with the paintbrush dipping it in the "ink" between each stroke. Then leave it to dry.

### Something to try

BALL-POINT PEN

To conceal the secret message, you can write another letter on top. Use a ball-point pen which will not run when you develop the invisible ink.

### Did you know?

In the past, prisoners of war made invisible ink from sweat and saliva. Like lemon juice, these become visible when you burn them.

## Developing the ink

With a clean teaspoon, put four teaspoons of washing soda in four tablespoons of hot water and stir until it has all dissolved.

**2** MESSAGE SIDE UPWARDS

Put about two teaspoons of warm water on a plate. Lay the paper with the message on the plate, so the paper absorbs the water.

**3** DO NOT TOUCH DROPS AFTER MESSAGE APPEARS

Now, very carefully put drops of washing soda solution on the paper with a teaspoon. Try and spread each drop out as it falls on the paper. You may have to practise this to get it right.

When you add the washing soda, the letters of the secret message should appear bright pink. The letters do not last very long though, as the colour runs into the washing soda solution.

### How it works

Phenolphthalein is an indicator, like the red cabbage water which you used to test for acids and alkalis. When you mix phenolphthalein with an alkali, such as washing soda, it turns pink.

# How to split water

Water is made from two chemicals joined together. The chemicals are called oxygen and hydrogen. In this experiment you can split water into oxygen and hydrogen with the electric current from a battery.

Oxygen and hydrogen belong to a group of chemicals called "elements" from which all substances are made. You can find out more about elements over the page.

You need two pencils sharpened at both ends, a 9 volt battery, 15 amp fuse wire, a jar of water, scissors, paper and sticky tape.

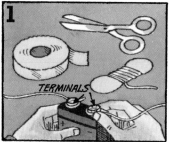

Cut two pieces of fuse wire about 20cm long and wind them round the metal terminals of the battery. Fix them with sticky tape.

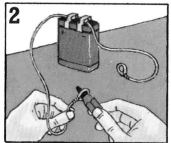

At the other end of each wire make a loop just big enough to fit round the lead point of a pencil.

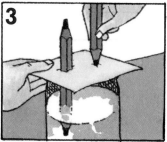

Rest a square of paper on the jar of water. Then push the pencils through it so they are held with their points in the water.

IF WIRES ARE NOT LONG ENOUGH STAND BATTERY ON BOOK

Loop the wires on to the lead points of the pencils. Then watch the pencil points in the water to see what happens.

## What happens

When you connect the battery wires to the pencil leads, the electric current from the battery flows along the wires and pencil leads and through the water.

As the current flows you should see bubbles forming round the points of the pencils. These are bubbles of oxygen and hydrogen gas. You can tell which bubbles are hydrogen and which are oxygen by looking at the battery terminals.

The oxygen collects round the pencil attached to the positive terminal (marked "+"). The hydrogen collects round the pencil attached to the negative terminal (marked "−"). Which pencil has the most bubbles round it?

### How it works

All substances are made of minute particles called atoms, and the atoms cling together in groups called molecules. Each water molecule contains two hydrogen atoms and one oxygen atom.

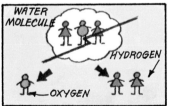

While the electric current flows the water molecules split up into atoms of hydrogen and oxygen. More hydrogen bubbles form because in water there are twice as many hydrogen atoms as oxygen.

# What are elements?

Elements are the basic chemicals from which all substances are made. There are only about 100 elements and all the millions of substances on Earth are made from different combinations of them.

A substance made from a combination of elements is called a compound. For example water is a compound and in the experiment on the previous page, you split it into hydrogen and oxygen, the elements of which it is made.

Some elements are well-known substances, such as gold, silver oxygen and carbon. Others are rare chemicals that are hardly ever seen.

Most of the things in this picture, including the human body, are made from compounds of only six different elements. Almost all the substances in the human body are made from different combinations of the elements oxygen, carbon, nitrogen, hydrogen, calcium and phosphorus. Hair, skin, muscles, wool and leather are all made from only four elements: oxygen, hydrogen, carbon and nitrogen.

## What ancient chemists thought

The Ancient Greeks thought there were only four elements: earth, air, fire and water, and that everything else in the world was made from these four things.

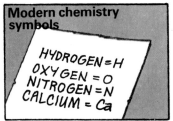

ALCHEMIST

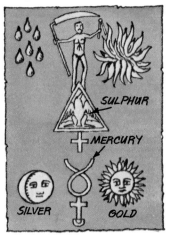

SULPHUR

MERCURY

SILVER

GOLD

Later, in the Middle Ages, people called alchemists believed they could turn ordinary metals to gold with a substance called the Philosopher's Stone. In their attempts to make the Stone they discovered a lot about the composition of different substances. They believed that sulphur, mercury and salt were the only three elements, and they wrote "recipes" for the Stone, using symbols for the elements and metals, as shown in the picture above.

### Modern chemistry symbols

HYDROGEN = H
OXYGEN = O
NITROGEN = N
CALCIUM = Ca

Chemists still use symbols for the elements. These are often the first letter or letters of the element's name. Chemists all over the world use the same symbols.

MOLECULE OF WATER

$= H_2O$

Compound substances are represented by the symbols of the elements they contain. So water is $H_2O$. The figure two shows there are two hydrogen atoms in each water molecule.

# Sorting out elements

Elements can be divided into two groups: metals, such as gold, iron and tin, and non-metals, such as hydrogen, oxygen and sulphur. The metal elements share certain characteristics. They can be polished to make them shine, they conduct electricity (that is, electricity can flow through them) and they are good conductors of heat. These qualities make them useful for lots of different purposes, as shown in these pictures.

The shiny surface of mirrors is made with a thin layer of silver on the back of the glass.

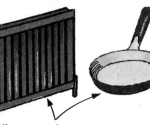

Radiators and cooking pans need to conduct heat, so they are made of metal.

Wires to carry electricity are usually made of copper, covered with plastic which does not conduct electricity.

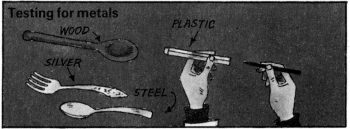

**Testing for metals**

WOOD

PLASTIC

SILVER

STEEL

You can usually tell when substances are metals, but some are not so easy to recognize. On the next few pages you can see how chemists identify metals by testing them to see if they conduct heat and electricity. For the tests you need some long thin objects, such as the things shown above, made from several different substances.

## Bean test for heat

This is a test which shows how well different substances conduct heat. You need things, such as those shown at the bottom of the opposite page, made of wood, steel, plastic and silver. If you do not have something silver, use another metal, such as a piece of copper pipe, or aluminium foil screwed into a long thin shape. You also need some dried beans (or peas), butter, hot water and a mug.

**1**

Put the things to be tested in the mug. Then use a tiny smear of butter to stick a bean on each thing.* Make sure all the beans are at the same height.

**2**

Fill the mug with boiling water and watch what happens. Note which objects lose their beans first.

Heat from the water travels up the objects and melts the butter so the beans fall off. The objects which lose their beans first are the ones through which heat travels fastest. These things are said to be good conductors of heat. You should find that the beans fall off the metal things first, showing that metals are good conductors of heat. There is another test over the page.

*The experiment will not work if you use too much butter.*

## Battery test

Here is a test to show that metals conduct electricity. You need a 4.5 volt battery, a 3.5 volt bulb, a miniature bulb holder,* three pieces of fuse wire 20cm long, and a very small screwdriver. You also need the objects you tested on the previous page.

Attach a piece of wire to each of the battery terminals. Then wind one of the wires round one of the screws on the bulb holder. Put the third piece of wire round the other screw on the bulb holder.

**2 IF BULB DOES NOT LIGHT, CHECK WIRES ARE FIRMLY CONNECTED**

If you hold the ends of the two loose wires together, the bulb should light. This shows there is an electric current flowing along the wires and through the bulb.

**3**

Now hold one of the objects you want to test between the two loose wires. Press the wires firmly on the object. If the electric current can flow through the substance of which the object is made, the bulb will light up.

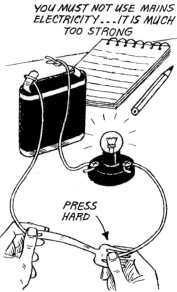

**YOU MUST NOT USE MAINS ELECTRICITY...IT IS MUCH TOO STRONG**

**PRESS HARD**

Test all the objects and note which of them conduct electricity. Then compare your results with those of the heat test. You should find that all the metal objects conduct electricity and heat.

*You can get these in electrical or hardware stores.*

## More things to test

### A pencil

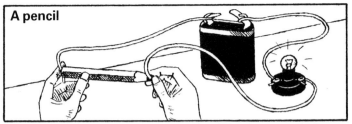

Try testing the lead in a pencil to see if it conducts electricity. Press one of the wires round the lead point of the pencil and the other against the lead on the flat end. The bulb should light up.

Pencil leads are made from an element called carbon. Carbon is an unusual element. It conducts electricity, but it does not have the other properties of metals, and it is not a metal.

### Salty water

Dissolve four teaspoons of salt in half a jar of warm water. Then dip the two wires into the salty water and see what happens.

YOU COULD TRY THIS TEST WITH WASHING SODA TOO

SALT

WASHING SODA

The bulb should glow faintly for a few seconds. This shows that the electric current from the two wires can flow through the salty water. The chemical name for salt is sodium chloride, and sodium is a metal. Anything that has a metal element in it conducts electricity when it is dissolved in water.

# Copperplating a key

In this experiment you can cover an old key, or other metal object, with copper. You need a chemical called copper sulphate, which you can buy at some chemists and toyshops.* Take great care with it, as it is poisonous. You also need a 4.5 volt battery, some thin copper electric wire, scissors, sticky tape, glasspaper and a teaspoon. You must *not* use a kitchen teaspoon, as copper sulphate is poisonous.

**1** SNIP DOUBLE STRANDED WIRE DOWN THE MIDDLE AND PULL APART

Cut two pieces of electric wire about 30cm long. Then, with scissors, strip off 3cm of the plastic at both ends of each wire.

**2** GLASSPAPER

Rub the key with glasspaper, then attach it to one of the wires.

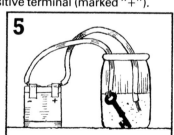

**3** FIX WIRE WITH STICKY TAPE

Look on the battery for the negative terminal (marked "−") and attach the wire with the key to it. Then attach the other wire to the positive terminal (marked "+").

**4**

Fill the jar one third full with water and stir in two teaspoons of copper sulphate. Remember, you must not use a kitchen teaspoon.

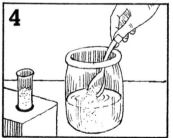

**5**

Dip the key and the other wire into the copper sulphate solution and leave it for about 20 minutes. Make sure the key does not touch the other wire.

118 *You can find out more about buying chemicals from toyshops on page 124.

## What happens

After about 20 minutes pull the key out and shake off any drops of copper sulphate into the jar. You should find the key has a pink coating of copper. This will turn orange if you leave it out in the air. You can find out how the copper is made below. If the key is not very well coated, put it back in the solution for a while.

*POUR THE COPPER SULPHATE DOWN THE LAVATORY WHEN YOU HAVE FINISHED*

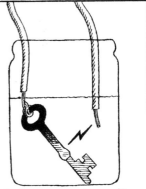

## If it does not work

Check that the wires are firmly attached to the battery terminals and that the wire from the key is attached to the negative terminal. If it still does not work, the battery may be flat. Test it in a torch, or just try the experiment again with a new battery.

## How the copper is made

When copper sulphate dissolves in water it splits into copper parts and sulphate parts. When you dip the key and the wire into the solution, an electric current flows through it and the copper parts are attracted to the negative battery terminal. They move towards the negative terminal and collect around the key. Some of the copper also comes from the wire attached to the positive terminal. This wire is eaten away by the current and the copper goes into the solution.

A similar process is used to put a thin coating of silver on jewellery and cutlery. This is called electroplating.

# Equipment to make

Here are some ideas for chemistry equipment you can make yourself. Below there is a test-tube rack for holding test-tubes. Opposite you can find out how to measure out drops of liquid with a drinking straw, and how to make a measuring jug.

Over the page there is another way to make gas-catching equipment and instructions for how to make limewater.

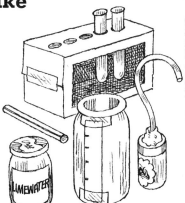

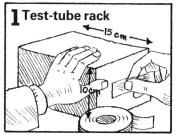

**1 Test-tube rack**

You need a small cardboard box about 10cm high and 15cm long. If the box opens at the ends, tape up the openings.

**2**

To cut out the front of the box, push the point of some scissors into the cardboard and make diagonal cuts to the corners. Do not cut right into the corners.

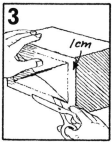

**3**

Then cut out the front of the box, leaving about 1cm round the edge.

**4**

Now, draw five or six circles along the top of the box, by drawing round the top of a test-tube. Cut out the circles to make the holes for the test-tubes.

## Drinking straw dropper

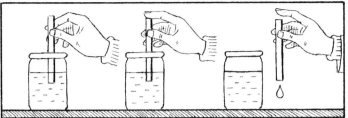

You need a wide, plastic straw. Cut a piece about 12cm long and dip it in some water. Then put your finger over the top and lift the straw out of the water. Some water is trapped inside.

To let one drop fall, lift your finger and replace it as soon as you see a drop forming on the end of the straw. You will need to practise until you can let just one drop fall at a time.

## Measuring jar for chemicals

To make this you need a large, straight-sided jar and a measuring jug.

Stick a strip of paper down the side of the jar. Then, with the measuring jug, pour 125ml of water into the jar. Mark the level on the strip of paper.

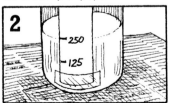

Empty the jar and label the mark 125ml. Then measure in 250ml and mark the water level again. Continue until you have all the measurements you want.

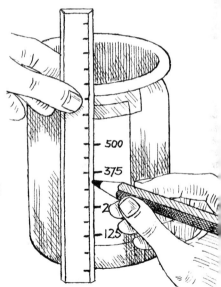

If you do not have a measuring jug, you can use a milk carton to pour 500ml of water into the jar.* Mark the level of the water, then empty the jar. Divide the distance below the mark into quarters.

*A milk carton holds 568ml so do not fill it right to the top.

## More gas-catching equipment

Here is a way to make gas-catching equipment for the gas tests if you do not have a test-tube. (If you have a test-tube you can make the equipment as shown on page 95.)

To make the equipment shown here you need some plasticine, a piece of plastic tubing about 40cm long, a blunt knife and a small container with a soft plastic lid (such as a pill box or a bubblebath container). It is best if the container is see-through, so you can see what is happening inside.

Push the point of the knife into the lid of the container, as shown above. Twist the knife round to make a hole just big enough for the plastic tubing to fit through.

Then push one end of the plastic tubing into the hole in the lid.

### How to use it

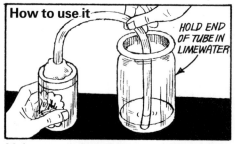

On the top of the lid press plasticine round the tube to seal any gaps.

Make a gas in the container as shown in the experiment you are doing. Then catch the gas by screwing the cap on as fast as you can.

# Making limewater

You may be able to buy limewater from a chemist, but if not, it is quite easy to make your own. You need a chemical called calcium hydroxide, which is also known as slaked lime.

## Where to get slaked lime

Test-tubes of slaked lime are sold as refills for chemistry sets, so you may be able to buy some from a toyshop (see page 124).

You can also buy slaked lime from a gardening shop. It is sold as "garden lime". Before you buy garden lime, though, check on the packet that it is made from calcium hydroxide or hydrated lime. Do not buy garden lime made from calcium carbonate or calcium oxide.

### 1 How to make it

CHEMISTRY SPOON

Put about three teaspoons of slaked lime in a jar and half-fill it with water.

### 2

Stir and leave it to settle for about four hours until the liquid clears.

### 3

Pour the clear limewater into a labelled jar and put the lid on.

### 4

You can make more limewater by adding water to the lime left in the bottom of the jar, stirring and leaving it to settle as before.

## Limewater check

If the limewater experiments do not work, it may be because the lime you used was not calcium hydroxide. You can check your limewater by blowing into it through a straw for a minute or two.* It should turn cloudy. If it does not, it is not proper limewater. You need to buy some more slaked lime. Make sure it is calcium hydroxide.

*Take care not to suck any of the liquid into your mouth.

# Buying chemicals

Most of the chemicals you need are household substances which you can buy from supermarkets. Below, there is a chart giving the chemical names of some common substances. Then there is a list showing where you can buy some of the more unusual ones. At the bottom of the page you can find out how to buy chemicals in chemists and toyshops.

## Chemical names

| | |
|---|---|
| Vinegar | Ethanoic acid |
| Lemon juice | Citric acid |
| Tea | Tannic acid |
| Sour milk | Lactic acid |
| Washing soda | Sodium carbonate |
| Bicarbonate of soda | Sodium hydrogen carbonate |
| Salt | Sodium chloride |
| Slaked lime | Calcium hydroxide |

## Where to buy chemicals

**Citric acid crystals** – Winemaking store

**Washing soda** – Hardware store

**Bicarbonate of soda** – Supermarket

**Cream of tartar** – Supermarket

**Slaked lime** – Toyshop, gardening shop

**Copper sulphate\*** – Toyshop, chemist

**Phenolphthalein** – Chemist (ask for laxative pills and check they contain this chemical).

**Distilled water** – Garage, chemist (you may have to take your own container).

**Iodine** – Chemist (ask for red tincture of iodine).

## Chemists

When you go to a chemist ask at the dispensary counter for the chemical you want and tell the assistant what it is for. Always take great care with chemicals, as they may be poisonous. Use them only in the way suggested in this book and wash them away as soon as you have finished.

## Toyshops

Toyshops sell small test-tubes of chemicals as refills for chemistry sets. If your toyshop does not stock these, you can write to a chemistry set manufacturer and ask them to send you the refills. To find the address, look on the box of a chemistry set, or ask in a toyshop.

*Copper sulphate is poisonous, so keep it in a jar marked "harmful".

# Where to buy equipment

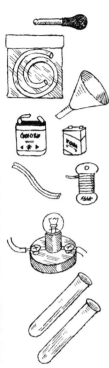

**Eyedropper** – You can buy one of these very cheaply from a chemist.

**Plastic tubing** – Also called syphon tubing. You can buy it at winemaking stores.

**Plastic funnel** – These are sold in hardware stores.

**Batteries** –You can buy batteries in electrical stores and many other kinds of stores.

**Fuse wire and copper electric wire** – These are sold in electrical and hardware stores.

**Miniature bulb holder and bulb** – Electrical and hardware stores sell these.

**Test-tubes** – Some toyshops sell test-tubes, or you can write to a chemistry set manufacturer and ask them to send you some. You could also look in the telephone book for the address of a laboratory supplier. They usually sell test-tubes in bulk, but if you phone them first, they may let you go to their warehouse to buy a few, or send you some by post. Ask for "pyrex" or "borosilicate glass" test-tubes, about 15cm long and 1.75cm diameter.

## Answer to chemical muddle puzzle (page 102)

This chart shows how each powder should react in the tests. Match your results with the chart in order to identify your five powders.

|  | Cream of tartar | Salt | Bicarbonate of soda | Flour | Sugar |
|---|---|---|---|---|---|
| Indicator test | Acid | Alkali | Alkali | Neutral | Neutral |
| Water test | Dissolved | Dissolved | Dissolved | Did not dissolve | Dissolved |
| Gas test | No gas | No gas | Carbon dioxide gas | No gas | No gas |

# Equipment lists

These two pages list all the things you need for the experiments. The experiments are grouped together by subject and all the equipment for each group of experiments is listed together. The numbers in brackets show the pages on which the experiments appear.

## Acid tests (74-79)
Knife
Wooden spoon
Teaspoon
Saucepan
Funnel
Paper towels
Bottle with a top
About 10 jars
Eyedropper*
Labels
Scissors
Pen
Notepad
Boiling water
Red cabbage (or rose petals or blackberries)
For testing:
Lemon juice
Orange juice
Tea
Bicarbonate of soda
Baking powder
Vinegar
Cola drink
Boiled sweet
Washing-up liquid
Washing soda
Liquid floor cleaner
Sour milk
Indigestion tablets
Milk of magnesia

## Water tests (80-83)
Distilled water
Tap water
Boiled water
Six jars
Teaspoon
Tablespoon
Grater (or knife)
Bar of soap
Washing soda
Eyedropper
Labels
Scissors
Notepad
Felt-tip pen

## How to make bath salts (84-85)
Washing soda
Cologne or perfume
Food colouring
Tablespoon
Rolling pin
Bowl
Polythene bag
Jar with lid
Saucer
Labels
Scissors
Pen

## Soap tests (86-87)
Three or four makes of washing powder
Butter or margarine
Warm water
Five jars
Teaspoon
Knife
Kitchen scales
Scissors
Rag
Labels
Pen
Notepad
Red cabbage indicator*

## Soap powder eats egg experiment (88-89)
Biological soap powder
Ordinary soap powder
Egg (hardboiled)
Tablespoon or measuring jar
Teaspoon
Knife
Scissors
Two jars
Labels
Pen

## Food tests (90-93)
Tincture of iodine
Jar
Test-tube (or jar)
Large mug
Saucer or jar lid
Teaspoon
Tablespoon
Eyedropper
Cold water
Boiling water
Flour
Newspaper
Clock or watch

Things to test:
Apple
Potato
Salt
Butter
Rice
Cheese
Meat
White paper
Paper glue
Laundry starch

## Making gas (95-99)
Three or four jars
Test-tube
Plastic tubing
Plasticine
Ruler
Scissors
Teaspoon
Drinking straw
Labels
Pen
Washing soda
Limewater (see page 95)
Vinegar

Some or all of the following:
A lemon
A grapefruit
Cola drink
Sour milk
continued above ▶

126 *This is useful, but not essential.

and some or all of these:
Bicarbonate of soda
Limestone or chalk from the ground (not blackboard chalk)
An eggshell

## Making fizzy drinks (100-101)
Bicarbonate of soda
Citric acid crystals
Icing sugar
A still drink
A bottle of fizzy drink
Kitchen teaspoon
Kitchen tablespoon
Bowl
Two jars with lids
Labels
Scissors
Pen
Gas-catching equipment (see page 95)
Limewater (see page 95)

## Chemical muddle puzzle (102-103)
Flour
Salt
Icing sugar
Bicarbonate of soda
Cream of tartar
Vinegar or other acid
Warm water
Teaspoon
Five jars
Five test-tubes (or five more jars)
Labels
Scissors
Pen
Notepad
Gas-catching equipment (see page 95)
Limewater (see page 95)
Red cabbage indicator (see page 74)

## Testing inks and dyes (104-106)
Four or five dark-coloured felt-tip pens
Two different black felt-tip pens
Blotting paper
Ruler
Scissors
Saucer
Jar
Water
Sugar-coated sweets (e.g. "Smarties")

## Invisible inks (107-109)
Paper
Paintbrush
Biro

For lemon juice ink:
Eggcup or small jar
Lemon
Clock or watch

For phenolphthalein ink:
Laxative pills containing phenolphthalein
Washing soda
Hot water
Two jars
Two teaspoons
Blunt knife
Tablespoon
Plate
Ruler

## How to split water (110-111)
Two pencils
Pencil sharpener
Ruler
Scissors
Paper
Sticky tape
A thick book
Jar
Water
9 volt battery
15 amp fuse wire

## Sorting out elements (114-117)
Long thin objects made from wood, plastic, steel, silver (or another metal, e.g. copper)
Notepad
Pen

For the heat test:
Dried beans or peas
Butter or margarine
Boiling water
Mug

For the battery test:
4.5 volt battery
15 amp fuse wire
3.5 volt bulb
Miniature bulb holder
Small screwdriver
Ruler
Scissors
Sticky tape
Pencil
Teaspoon
Jar
Water
Salt

## Copperplating a key (118-119)
Old key or other metal object
Copper sulphate
Glasspaper
4.5 volt battery
Thin copper electric wire
Scissors
Ruler
Sticky tape
Teaspoon (not a kitchen one)
Jar
Water
Clock or watch

# Index

# FUN WITH ELECTRONICS

# Fun with electronics

Electronics consultant: Martin Owen
Technical advice by Jaqo
Lettering and circuit diagrams by J. G. McPherson

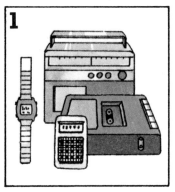

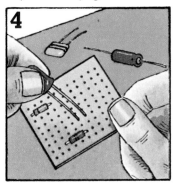

Electronics is the very careful and precise control of tiny electric currents. Digital watches, transistor radios, calculators, tape recorders and computers all work by means of electronics.

This part of the book shows you how to build lots of electronic things. Over the page you can find out about the things you need, and you can find out where to buy them on page 188.

On the next few pages there are some tests you can do to find out how electronics works. Then there are some general instructions showing you how to build electronic equipment. You need to read these instructions before you tackle the projects.

When you are building electronic things you have to be very careful and accurate. If one tiny thing is in the wrong place, the project will not work. Do not worry, though, if your projects do not work at first. There is a checklist to help you find the faults on page 192.

# Things you need

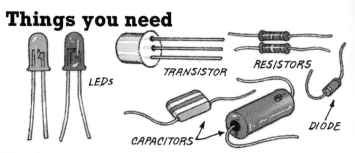

LEDs

TRANSISTOR

RESISTORS

CAPACITORS

DIODE

To build the projects you need tiny things called electronic components. They are very small and cheap and you can find out where to get them at the bottom of the page.

The components control the current in various ways. You will find out more about them as you read through the book.

VEROBOARD

For each project you have to connect the components together in a certain way, called a circuit. The way the current flows through the circuit is what makes the project work.

To build a circuit you solder the components to special board called Veroboard. You can find out how to do this, and how to solder, in the general instructions later in the book.

### Buying components and board

You can buy components and Veroboard at electronics components shops. If you have problems finding any parts you can write to either of the suppliers on page 192.

There is more advice about buying components on page 188, and a complete list of the components you need for all the projects and tests in this book.

## Equipment

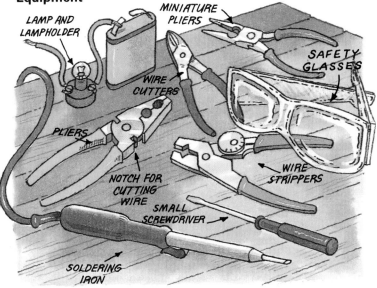

LAMP AND LAMPHOLDER

MINIATURE PLIERS

SAFETY GLASSES

WIRE CUTTERS

PLIERS

NOTCH FOR CUTTING WIRE

WIRE STRIPPERS

SMALL SCREWDRIVER

SOLDERING IRON

You will need a very small screwdriver and a pair of miniature pliers. Wire strippers are useful for taking the plastic cover off wires, but you can use pliers or scissors instead. You also need a pair of wire cutters, or ordinary pliers with a wire cutter on the side, a soldering iron and safety glasses.

## Battery power

NEVER USE THE ELECTRICITY IN YOUR HOUSE FOR THE PROJECTS. THE VOLTAGE IS MUCH TOO STRONG. IT WOULD GIVE YOU A VERY BAD SHOCK AND COULD EVEN KILL YOU.

All the projects in this book work on the electric current from a battery. Never connect any of the projects to the electricity in the plugs in your house. The voltage from these plugs is much too strong. It would burn out all the components in the project and could easily kill you.

# How electronics works

An electric current is created by a flow of minute particles called electrons. Electronic equipment works by controlling and using these electrons.

Electrons are part of the atoms of which everything in the world is made. This book and everything else around you is made of millions of invisibly small atoms.

**Atoms and electrons**

*NUCLEUS*

*ELECTRONS*

There are lots of different kinds of atoms, and every atom has a nucleus in the middle, with electrons spinning round it.

Each electron carries a tiny bit of electricity called a negative charge. The nucleus has a positive charge of electricity.

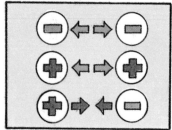

Charges of positive and negative electricity are attracted to each other, and charges which are the same (e.g. two negative charges), move away from each other.

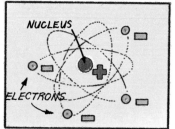

*NUCLEUS*

*ELECTRONS*

The electrons, which are negatively charged, usually stay spinning round the nucleus because they are attracted by the positive charge of the nucleus.

## Making current

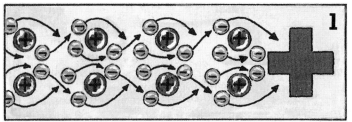

**1**

If there is a stronger positive charge nearby, the electrons in some substances will leave their nuclei and flow towards the stronger positive charge. This flow of electrons creates an electric current. The electrons in metals move easily, and metals are said to be good conductors of electricity. Electrons in plastic do not move, so electric current cannot flow through plastic.*

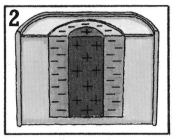

**2**

To make the electrons move you can use a battery. The battery contains a supply of strong positive and negative electric charges.

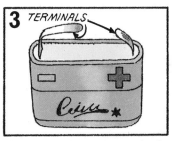

**3** TERMINALS

The battery has two terminals. One terminal is connected to the positively charged part of the battery and the other to the negatively charged part.

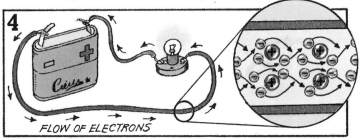

**4**

FLOW OF ELECTRONS

If you connect a piece of wire to the positive and negative battery terminals, the electrons in the wire will flow towards the positive charge in the battery. In this picture the wires are also connected to a bulb. The bulb lights up and this shows that the movement of the electrons is an electric current.

*This is why electric wires are made of metal covered with plastic.* 135

# Batteries, wire and lamps

This page shows the batteries, wire and lamps you can use. Opposite, you can find out how to fix wire to batteries.

## Batteries

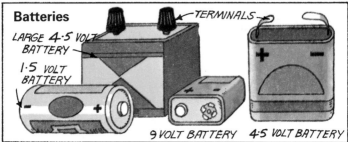

LARGE 4·5 VOLT BATTERY

1·5 VOLT BATTERY

TERMINALS

9 VOLT BATTERY

4·5 VOLT BATTERY

The force in the battery which makes the electrons move is called the voltage, and the strength of the battery is measured in volts. Some of the projects in this book need a 4.5 volt battery and others need a 9 volt battery.

Batteries come in lots of shapes and sizes and there are several different types of terminals. It does not matter which you use as long as it is the right voltage.

## Electric wire

SOLID CORE

STRANDED

TWIN CABLE

This has a core of metal to carry the electric current. It is covered with plastic. Some electric wire has a solid core of metal, others have strands of metal inside. It does not matter which you buy, but thin wire, such as "bell wire" and stranded wire, is easiest to use. If you have "twin cable", split it by cutting the case between the wires, then pull the wires apart.

## Lamps

You will need several small screw-in bulbs, like these, which are called "lamps" in electronics, and some miniature "lamp holders" to put them in.

Lamps are made in different strengths for using with different voltages of battery. Always use 6 volt lamps with a 9 volt battery and 3.5 volt lamps with a 4.5 volt battery.

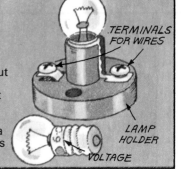

TERMINALS FOR WIRES

LAMP HOLDER

VOLTAGE

## Stripping wire

**1**

You have to remove 1.5cm of the plastic from each end of a piece of wire.

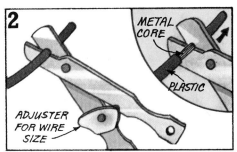

**2**

METAL CORE

PLASTIC

ADJUSTER FOR WIRE SIZE

If you use wire strippers, set the strippers so they cut through the plastic, but not through the metal core. Grip the wire in the strippers, about 1.5cm from the end, and firmly pull the plastic case off the metal.

**3**

SCORE

If you are careful, you can strip wire with scissors. Grip the wire in the scissors and twist, so the scissors score the plastic. Then pull the plastic off.

### Fixing wire to batteries

SOLDER WIRES TO HOLDER

CLIP-ON CONNECTOR

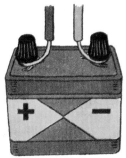

These pictures show how to fix wires to the various types of terminals on batteries. If you use stranded wire, twist the strands together in your fingers, so the wire is easier to handle.

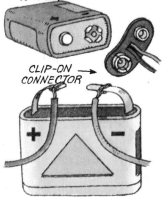

If you use round batteries, you will need a battery holder to put them in. You can buy one, or take one out of an old radio. You can also use sticky tape to hold batteries and wire together.

# Battery and lamp experiments

Here are some experiments you can do with a battery and lamps to find out more about how current flows. You need a 4.5 volt battery, two 3.5 volt lamps, two lamp holders and two pieces of wire about 25cm long. Before you start, strip the plastic case off the ends of the wires, as shown on the previous page.

**1**

TERMINALS

Twist one end of each wire firmly round the battery terminals.

**2**

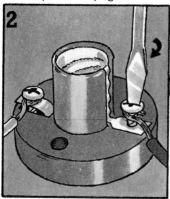

Loosen the screws on the lamp holder and twist the other ends of the wires clockwise round the screws. Tighten the screws.

**3**

Now screw a lamp into the lamp holder. If it does not light up, check that the wires are firmly connected to the battery and lamp holder.

**4**

NEGATIVE TERMINAL

Try taking the wire off the negative battery terminal. The lamp goes out. This shows that the positive charge by itself cannot make the electrons move.

**5**

Now touch the negative terminal with the wire again. For current to flow there has to be a complete link, called a circuit, from the negative to the positive part of the battery.

## How lamps work

Inside a lamp there is a very thin wire called a filament, through which the electric current has to pass. The filament is so thin that it is difficult for all the electrons to flow through it.

As the electrons squeeze through the filament, the wire becomes white hot and gives off light. The way the wire restricts the flow of electrons is called resistance.

### Another experiment

Now try setting up a battery like this, with two 3.5 volt lamps linked by a piece of wire. What happens to the light from the lamps this time?

With two lamps in the circuit there is twice as much resistance to the flow of electrons as there was with only one lamp. This reduces the amount of current in the wires, so the lamps are dimmer.

### Measures of electricity

The force in the battery which makes the electrons move is called the **voltage.** It is measured in **volts,** written **V** for short.

The amount of current that flows through the wires is measured in **amperes,** written **amps** or **A** for short.

The amount of resistance to the flow of electrons is measured in **ohms,** written Ω for short.* **K**Ω is used for 1,000 ohms.

*Ω is the sign for the Greek letter omega.

# Circuit diagrams

A circuit diagram is a drawing which shows how the components in a circuit are connected. Each component is shown by a symbol. The symbols for lamps, batteries and wires are shown here, and there are also some simple circuits to build.

The circuit diagrams for the projects in this book are on pages 186–187. You do not have to use the diagrams, though, to build the projects.

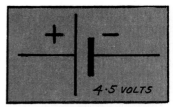

This is the symbol for a battery. The thin line is the positive (+ve) terminal and the shorter, thicker one is the negative (−ve) terminal. The strength of the battery is written beside the symbol.

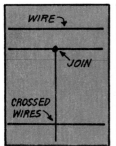

Wires are shown as straight lines and a dot shows where wires are joined.

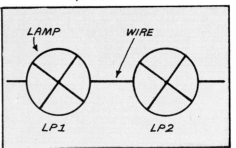

Lamps are shown like this, with the straight lines between them showing the wires. Each of the components in a circuit is labelled with its initial and number.

## Circuit diagram

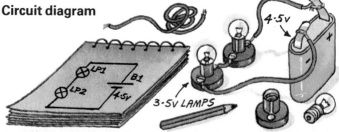

This is the diagram for the lamps and battery circuit shown here. When the lamps are placed like this, one after the other on the same piece of wire, it is called a "series circuit". Try

building the circuit, then unscrew one of the lamps. This makes a break in the circuit so the other lamp goes out as it is no longer linked to both the battery terminals.

## More circuits to build

See if you can build the circuits shown below, following the diagrams.

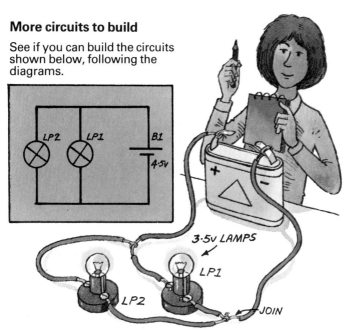

This circuit has two lamps on separate loops of wire. It is called a "parallel circuit". Try undoing one of the lamps. The other lamp stays alight as there is still a complete circuit to and from the battery. The lamps in this circuit are brighter than those in the series circuit because the same amount of current from the battery flows along each loop of wire. In the series circuit, both the lamps are resisting the current on the same piece of wire, so they both receive less current.

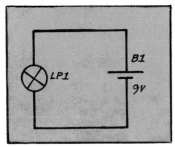

This diagram shows that the circuit needs a 9 volt battery. If you do not have one you can link two 4.5 volt batteries in a series circuit as shown in the

picture above. The negative terminal of one battery should be linked to the positive terminal of the other battery.

# Electronic components

These two pages show the electronic components you will be using to build the projects. You can find out more about them on pages 176-183 , and there are also some tests to show how they work. It is a good idea to do some of the tests before you build the projects, so you get used to handling the components and can see how they work.

The components you buy may not look exactly the same as the ones shown here and in the projects, as there are lots of different kinds which do the same job. On pages 190-191 there are some clues to help you sort out your components for the projects.

### Resistors

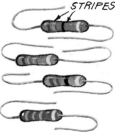

STRIPES

These reduce the amount of current in the circuit by resisting the flow of the electricity. The strength of each resistor, that is, its resistance, is measured in ohms (written $\Omega$, or K$\Omega$ for 1,000 ohms). The resistance is marked on each resistor with a code of coloured stripes. In the projects, resistors are referred to by the colours of their stripes. You can find out how to read the colours at the bottom of the opposite page and the code is explained on page 177.

### Variable resistors

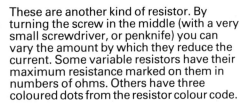

SCREW

COLOUR CODE

These are another kind of resistor. By turning the screw in the middle (with a very small screwdriver, or penknife) you can vary the amount by which they reduce the current. Some variable resistors have their maximum resistance marked on them in numbers of ohms. Others have three coloured dots from the resistor colour code.

### Diodes

Diodes are rather like one-way streets – the current can flow through them one way but not the other. You have to be careful to connect them correctly and there is a stripe on one end of the diode to show you how.

### Light emitting diodes or LEDs

FLAT EDGE

These glow like tiny bulbs and, like diodes, the current can only flow through them one way. The base of the case of an LED has a flat edge to help you identify the legs. You have to look carefully to see it. The project instructions tell you where to put the leg nearest the flat edge.

### Transistors

TAG

Transistors can control the strength of the current in the circuit, and can also switch it off and on. You have to be careful to connect transistors correctly as they can be damaged if the current flows through them the wrong way. Each transistor has one leg marked with a coloured spot or metal tag on the case, and the instructions for the projects tell you exactly where to put the legs.

### Capacitors

+ SIGNS

These components store a small amount of electricity, measured in microfarads (written μF)* or, for very small amounts, picofarads (pF). Some capacitors, called "electrolytic capacitors", have + or − signs on one end and these must be connected the right way in the circuit. The project instructions show you how.

### Audio transformer

This changes electric current to make it the best kind of current for a loudspeaker or crystal earpiece.

### Other things

YOUR SWITCH AND SOCKET MAY LOOK DIFFERENT FROM THESE

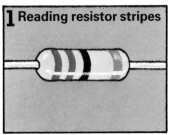

LOUDSPEAKER

CRYSTAL EARPIECE

SWITCH

MINIATURE SOCKET AND PLUG

## 1 Reading resistor stripes

## 2

RED, RED, BLACK RESISTOR

Each resistor has three coloured stripes at one end, and a gold, silver, red or brown one near the other end.

To identify a resistor, hold it with the three stripes on the left, then read the colours from left to right. To find out what the colours mean, see page 177.

*μ is the sign for the Greek letter "m", called mu.

# General instructions
## How to build the projects

To build the projects you connect the components together on special board called Veroboard. This has rows of holes in it, with strips of copper on the back linking the holes. You fit the components through the holes and the electric current flows to them along the copper tracks.

When you buy Veroboard, ask for board with copper strips, and with holes 0.1in apart.*

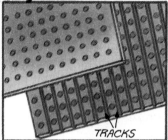

TRACKS

In this book the front of a piece of board is called the "plainside" and the back, with the copper tracks on it, is called the "trackside".

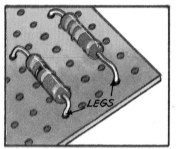

LEGS

You fit the components through the holes like this, then solder their legs to the tracks. You can find out how to solder over the page.

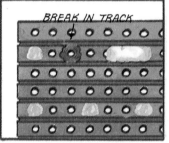

BREAK IN TRACK

The current flows through all the components soldered to the same track. Sometimes you have to redirect the current by breaking the track.

DRILL BIT

You can break the track with a drill bit held in your fingers. Use about a 4.5mm bit and turn it to remove all the copper.

HOLD RULER FIRMLY

To cut board, score it several times on the trackside with a sharp knife (e.g. penknife) and metal ruler. Then break it.

*This is the distance between two holes, measured from the centres of the holes.

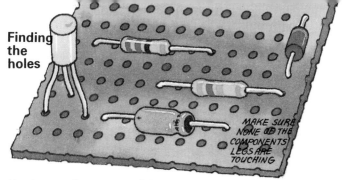

**Finding the holes**

MAKE SURE NONE OF THE COMPONENTS LEGS ARE TOUCHING

You have to be very careful to put all the components in the correct holes. In the projects each hole is called by a letter and number. The letter shows which track it is in and the number shows how many holes it is along the track. The board must be plainside up when finding the holes and tracks. To help you find the holes you can draw a grid.

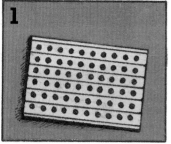

Cut the board to the size for the project. The size is given as the number of tracks by the number of holes along a track (e.g. 6 tracks x 10 holes).

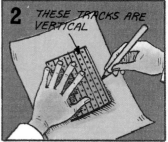

THESE TRACKS ARE VERTICAL

Put the board on a piece of paper with the tracks either horizontal or vertical as indicated in the project. Draw round the board.

TRACKSIDE

Make marks for the tracks along one edge of the board and for the holes along another edge.

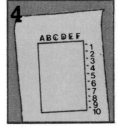

ABCDEF

Label the tracks with letters and the holes with numbers as shown in each project.

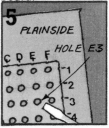

PLAINSIDE

HOLE E3

To find a hole, put the board on the grid plainside up, and read off its letter and number.

# How to solder

Soldering is a way of joining two pieces of metal, using melted metal called solder. It makes a firm joint through which the electric current can flow.

When the soldering iron is on, do not touch the bit as it is very hot. Keep the wire of the soldering iron out of your way so there is no danger of burning it with the bit.

Always wear safety glasses when soldering or cutting component wires.

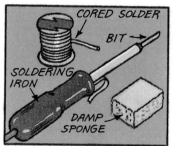

These are the things you will need. "Cored" solder has a substance in it that makes it flow easily when it melts.

**Soldering a component**

PROP IRON UP CAREFULLY

Plug the iron in and wait for it to heat up. Prop it up so the bit is not touching anything.

Find the right holes for the component. You can mark them with a felt-tip pen.

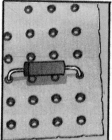

Put the legs of the component through the holes, like this.

LEGS

Bend the legs out slightly at the back, to hold the component in place.

Wipe the bit on the damp sponge to remove old solder.

Touch the hot bit with solder so a drop clings to it to "wet" it.

146

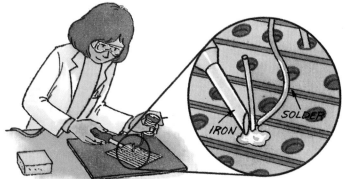

Then, both at the same time, put the tip of the solder wire and the bit on the place where the component's leg touches the track. Leave them there for just a second, to avoid overheating. There should be a small amount of solder joining the leg to the track. Let the joint cool for a few seconds.

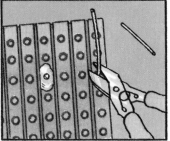

With wire cutters, trim the legs close to the solder. *Tilt the board away from you and put your finger on the leg to stop it flying up out of the cutters.*\*

REMOVE SOLDER BETWEEN TRACKS AS SHOWN BELOW

The joints should be smooth and shiny and there must not be any solder between the tracks. This would let the current flow from track to track.

To remove solder between tracks, run the hot iron along in the groove.

WHEN YOU HAVE FINISHED SOLDERING REMEMBER TO UNPLUG THE SOLDERING IRON.

If you want to remove a joint, hold the board like this, put the hot iron on the joint and flick the solder towards the table. Be careful as the molten solder is hot.

*\*Be very careful doing this as the pieces of metal can fly a long way.* 147

# More soldering

## 1 Wires

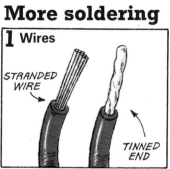

STRANDED WIRE

TINNED END

If you use stranded wire you should cover the strands with solder to hold them together. This is called "tinning".

## 2

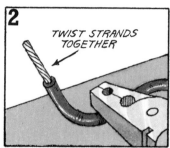

TWIST STRANDS TOGETHER

Strip 1cm of the plastic off the wire, then twist the strands together. Put something on the wire to hold it steady while you tin it.

## 3

CLEAN BIT ON SPONGE

Heat the soldering iron, then clean the bit and "wet" it with solder as before.

## 4

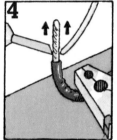

Then quickly stroke the wire with the bit and the solder at the same time.

## 5

STRANDS SHOWING THROUGH SOLDER

The tinned wire should be lightly coated with solder, like this.

## Wire links

LINK BETWEEN TRACKS

Sometimes you need to carry the current from one track to another by linking them with a piece of wire.

SHORT LINK

You can use stranded or solid core wire for links. For very short ones you can use pieces of metal paper clip.

## Fixing wires to the board

You can solder wire links straight to the track, but other wires should be soldered to pins which are soldered to the board.

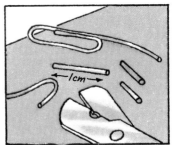

For pins, use pieces about 1cm long cut from metal paper clips, or thick pieces of wire cut off the legs of components.

### Fixing pins

Put the pin in the hole so about 7mm shows on the plainside of board. Solder to track.

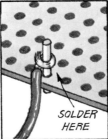

With the board plainside up, wind a piece of wire round the pin, then solder it to the pin.

### Hint

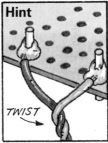

You can twist two wires together, like this, to keep them tidy.

### Board holder

Two blocks of wood with grooves in like this, are useful for holding the board while you solder the components.

Clamp the wood in a vice while you saw the grooves. They must be wide enough to take the thickness of the Veroboard.

149

# Hints for success

Before you build any of the circuits it is a good idea to practise soldering some pieces – you will find it much easier after a bit of practice. Make sure you have all the correct components for the project you want to build. There are some clues to help you identify them on page 190. Here are some other points to remember.

**1** Remember that the letter for each hole shows which track it is in and the number shows how many holes it is along the track.

**2** Take great care to put the legs of the transistors in the correct holes, and to place electrolytic capacitors the right way round.

**3** Check each soldered joint (when it is cool) to make sure it is firm and shiny. If it is not, resolder it. Make sure there is no solder between the tracks.

**4** Make sure the legs of the components are not touching each other on the plainside.

**5** Before you connect the battery, check your board against the project pictures to make sure *all* the components are in the right holes.

**6** Make sure you connect the wires from the board to the battery correctly.

**7** If the project does not work, turn to the faults checklist at the end of the book. In electronics you often have to check a project several times before you can get it to work.

## Boxing the projects

If you like, you can put the projects in boxes. You should decide how you are going to box a project before you build it.*

You may need to lengthen the legs of LEDs so they show outside the box. You can do this by soldering pieces of wire to them.

150   *There are ideas for boxing the projects on pages 184-185.*

# Things to make
# Guessing game

This game has two lights and when you press the switch, one of the lights comes on. You can never tell which one will light up. You could play it with friends, asking them to guess which light will come on, and see who gets it right most often.

GAME IN BOX

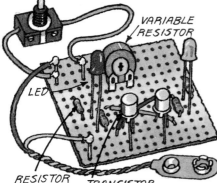

VARIABLE RESISTOR

LED

RESISTOR  TRANSISTOR

For hints on identifying the components, see page 190.

## Parts list

Two 390Ω* resistors (orange, white, brown)
Two 82KΩ resistors (grey, red, orange)
1KΩ variable resistor (vertical skeleton type)
Two transistors type BC107
Two LEDs
Pushbutton on/off switch
60cm electric wire
Three pins
Veroboard 13 tracks x 15 holes
9 volt battery and clip connector

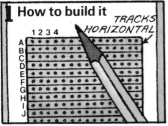

### 1 How to build it

TRACKS HORIZONTAL

Put the Veroboard, tracks horizontal, on a piece of paper. Draw a grid (see page 145). Label the tracks A-M and number the holes.

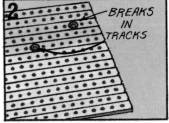

### 2

BREAKS IN TRACKS

Turn the Veroboard plainside up on the grid. Break the track (with a drill bit between your fingers) in holes C3 and E8.

*Ω means ohm and KΩ means 1,000 ohm.

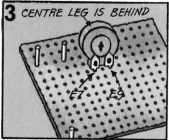

**3** CENTRE LEG IS BEHIND

E7    E9

Solder the three pins in holes C1, C4 and M1. Then solder the variable resistor with its centre leg in C8 and the other two in E7 and E9, as above.

**4**

Solder one of the grey, red, orange resistors (82KΩ) in holes G4, J4, and the other grey, red, orange one in G13, J13. The board should now look like this.

**5**

Solder the orange, white, brown resistors (390Ω) in holes E2, H2 and E15, H15. Check all the joints so far to make sure they are firm and shiny.

**6** NEGATIVE LEGS

The LEDs go in holes H3, J3 and H14, J14. On each, the negative leg should be in track J. (To find the negative leg see page 181.)

**7**

Now break the track in holes G8, H8, J8 and K8.

**8** FLAT EDGE

TRACK M

TAGS

One transistor goes in holes J6, K7, M6 and the other in J10, K11, M10. Make sure that on each transistor the leg nearest the metal tag is in track M.

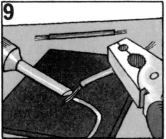

**9**

Cut two pieces of wire 4cm long. Strip 0.5cm of the plastic case off each end of both wires. If it is stranded wire, tin the ends with solder, as shown above.

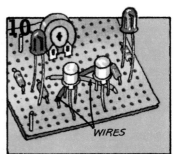

**10**

WIRES

Put one of the pieces of wire in holes G5, K12 and the other in K5, G12, so they cross over as in the picture. Solder the wires in position.

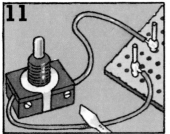

**11**

Solder two wires, 8cm long, to pins C1 and C4. Put the other ends of the wires in the holes in the switch and tighten the screws.*

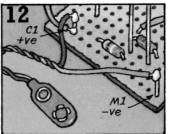

**12**

C1
+ve

M1
–ve

Now solder wires for the battery to pins C1 and M1. If you use a clip connector the red wire (positive) must go to C1.

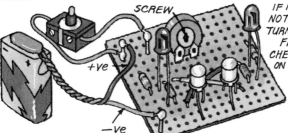

SCREW

+ve

–ve

IF IT DOES NOT WORK, TURN TO THE FAULTS CHECKLIST ON PAGE 192

Then connect the battery and press the switch a few times to test the circuit. If one LED lights up much more often than the other, adjust the variable resistor by turning the screw in the centre with a screwdriver or penknife. Keep adjusting the screw a tiny amount until both LEDs are working.

*If your switch is different from this one, see page 188.     153

# Pot plant tester

You can use this little electronic device to see if a pot plant needs watering. It has only three electronic components and is quite easy to build. The finished board is shown below.

VARIABLE RESISTOR

TRANSISTOR

LED    PROBES

To test a plant you stick the long probes into the earth. If the LED stays on it means the soil is dry and the plant needs watering. If the light flickers, or goes off, the soil is still damp.

## Parts list

4.7KΩ variable resistor (vertical skeleton type)
Transistor type BC171A
LED (any colour)
Two pieces of stiff wire 10cm long (you can use straightened paper clips) for the probes
20cm plastic sleeving to cover probes (size 2mm bore) or use sticky tape
20cm electric wire
Two pins
4.5 volt battery
Veroboard 7 tracks x 12 holes

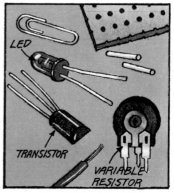

LED

TRANSISTOR

VARIABLE RESISTOR

154

# How to make the pot plant tester

Trackside up, put the board on a piece of paper with the tracks running vertically. On the paper label tracks A-G and number the holes.

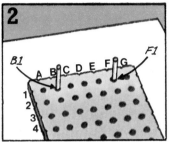

Turn the board plainside up on the grid. Put a pin in hole B1 and hole F1. Turn the board over and solder the pins to the tracks.

Cover the probes with casing or sticky tape, leaving 1cm bare at both ends of each wire.

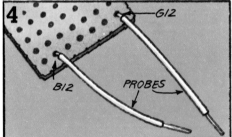

With pliers, bend one end of each probe to make a right angle. Then solder the probes in holes B12 and G12, so they look like this.

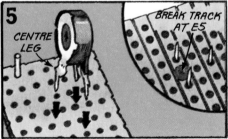

Break the track in hole E5. The variable resistor goes in holes C5, E4 and E6, with the centre leg in C5. Solder the legs to the back of the board.

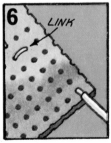

Now solder a short metal link from E7 to F7. You can use a piece of paperclip.

**7**

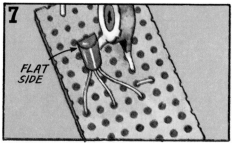

FLAT SIDE

Hold the transistor upright with the flat side facing the variable resistor and put the legs in holes A8, C8 and E8, as shown above. Make sure the flat side is facing the variable resistor.*

**8**

LINK

Strip the plastic off the ends of a short piece of wire and solder it in holes C9 and G9.

**9**

FLAT EDGE

B10

Examine the LED to find the negative leg. (To find out how to do this turn to page 181.) Put the LED in holes A10 and B10, with the negative leg in B10.

**10**

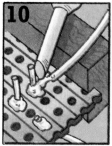

Solder the LED to the board then trim off the legs at the back.

**11**

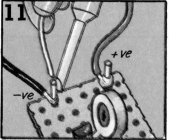

+ve

−ve

Now solder two 8cm pieces of wire to pins B1 and F1 for the battery. B1 is the negative wire and F1 is the positive wire.

**12**

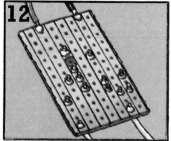

Before you connect the battery, make sure all the pieces are in the right holes and that there is no solder between the tracks.

**156** *If your transistor has a tag, the leg nearest the tag goes in hole A8.

## Testing it

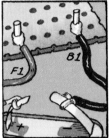

Connect the battery (B1 to negative and F1 to positive). The LED should light up.

Now, if you put the two probes on a piece of damp cloth, the LED should go out. If it stays on, adjust the variable resistor by turning the screw in the centre, until the LED goes out.

### How it works

IF IT DOES NOT WORK, TURN TO THE FAULTS CHECKLIST ON PAGE 192

Water is a good conductor of electricity, so when the soil is wet, the current can flow between the two probes. When the current flows this way through the circuit, the transistor switches off and the LED goes out. When the soil is dry, the current cannot pass between the probes and the LED stays on.

### Useful clips

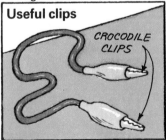

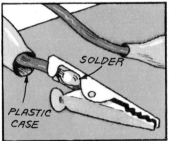

A length of wire with crocodile clips like these on the ends, is useful for connecting a circuit to a battery.

You can buy these clips in electrical stores, and solder them to a short piece of wire.

157

# How to make a burglar alarm

When this electronic alarm goes off it makes a loud squeaky noise. You could put it on the door of your room, or on a private cupboard, and when someone opens the door, the alarm will go off.

The board with all the components on is shown below.

MAGNET
ALARM

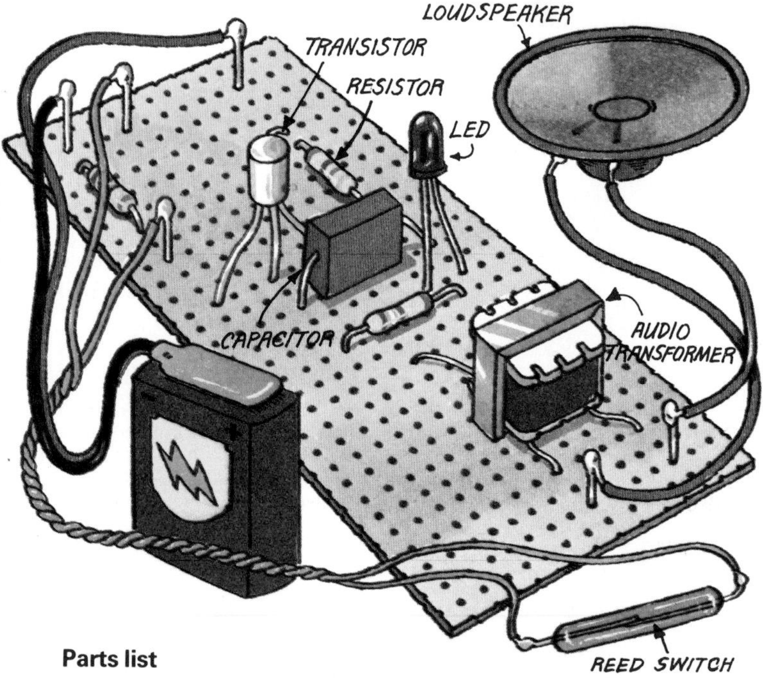

LOUDSPEAKER
TRANSISTOR
RESISTOR
LED
CAPACITOR
AUDIO TRANSFORMER
REED SWITCH

## Parts list

22 Ω resistor (red, red, black)
4.7KΩ resistor (yellow, violet, red)
39KΩ resistor (orange, white, orange)
Transistor type AC127
Audio transformer type LT700
0.01μF capacitor *
8Ω miniature loudspeaker
LED (any colour)

Reed switch (normally open type)
Magnet (any kind)
Six pins
9 volt battery and clip connector
Veroboard 14 tracks x 30 holes
Electric wire (enough to reach from the door to where you place the alarm)

158    *Your capacitor may have brown, black, orange and red stripes.

## How to build the alarm

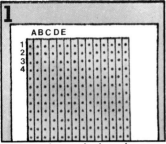

With tracks vertical, make a grid on a piece of paper. Turn board onto the plainside and find B2, E2, K2, B9, H29 and L29. Solder pins in these holes.

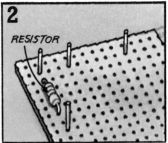

RESISTOR

Break the track in holes B5, K9, H25 and L25. Then put the red, red black resistor (22Ω) in holes B3, B7.

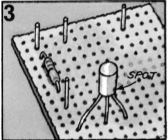

SPOT

The transistor goes in holes B12, E12 and G12. The leg nearest the spot or tag on the case must go in hole G12.

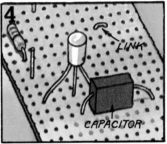

LINK

CAPACITOR

Put the capacitor in E14, L14. It does not matter which leg goes in which hole. Next, solder a wire link from J5 to K5. You can use a piece of paperclip for this.

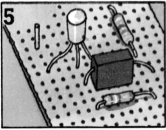

The yellow, violet, red resistor (4.7KΩ) goes in K6 and K12 and the orange, white, orange one (39KΩ) in E17 and K17.

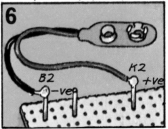

B2 —ve    K2 +ve

Now solder the battery clip wires to the pins in B2 and K2. The red wire (positive) must go to K2 and the other wire (negative) to B2.

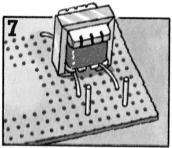

**7**

The audio transformer has two thick metal legs. You do not need these, so bend them up flat under it, then solder its wire legs in holes G19, J19, L19, H27 and L27.

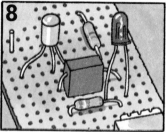

**8**

Put the LED in J16 and L16. The negative leg must go in J16. (To find the negative leg see page 181.)

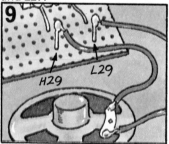

**9**

Solder two short wires to pins H29 and L29. Then solder the other ends of the wires to the terminals on the back of the loudspeaker.

**10**

Now cut two lengths of wire long enough to reach from the door to where you are going to hide the circuit board and speaker.

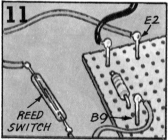

**11**

Solder one end of each wire to each end of the reed switch, and the other ends to pins B9 and E2.

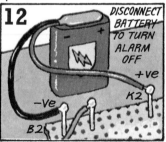

**12**

Now, if you connect the battery the alarm should go off. B2 is the negative wire and K2 is the positive.

## Setting up the alarm

Stick the reed switch on the door frame, very close to the door, using masking tape or insulating tape which will not spoil the paintwork.

TAPE

REED SWITCH

MAGNET *

Tape the magnet on the door, about 10mm in from the edge, and exactly opposite the reed switch.

HIDE THE WIRE UNDER THE CARPET OR TAPE IT TO THE SKIRTING BOARD

IF IT DOES NOT WORK, TURN TO THE FAULTS CHECKLIST ON PAGE 192

Now connect the battery, then open the door and the alarm should go off. To stop the alarm, close the door or remove the battery. If it does not work, try moving the magnet and reed switch a little bit closer to each other. The circuit is controlled by the reed switch, and the reed switch is operated by the magnet.

*This is a bar magnet, but any kind of magnet will do.

# Shaky hand game

Here is a game you can make to test how steady your hands are. You have to take the handle from one end of the metal loop to the other, without letting it touch the metal. If it does, the buzzer goes off and you are out.

There is a large picture of the finished board with all the components on over the page.

TWIST WIRES TOGETHER TO KEEP THEM TIDY

METAL LOOP

HANDLE

## Parts list

22Ω resistor (red, red, black)
4.7KΩ resistor (yellow, violet, red)
27KΩ resistor (red, violet, orange)
Transistor type BFY50
0.22μF capacitor
Audio transformer type LT700
8Ω miniature loudspeaker (you can use the same loudspeaker for all the projects)
LED (any colour)
5 pins
Veroboard 20 tracks x 27 holes
9 volt battery and clip connector

You also need about 1.5m of electric wire to attach to the handle and loudspeaker. The metal loop and handle are made of tinned copper wire. This comes in various thicknesses, so ask for 50cm of s.w.g. (standard wire gauge) 20. You can cover the handle with sticky tape, or buy special plastic sleeving for it. You would need about 12cm of 2mm bore sleeving.

# How to build the shaky hand game

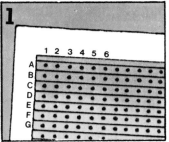

Draw a grid with the tracks running horizontally. Label the tracks A-T. Break the track in holes C7, C12, P20, R11.

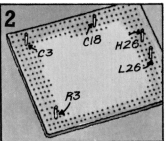

Solder the five pins in holes C3, C18, H26, L26 and R3. Remember to count the holes on the plainside of the board.

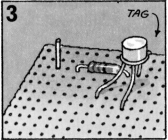

Fit the red, red, black resistor (22Ω) in C5 and C10 and the transistor in F8, C11 and G11. The leg nearest the tag must be in C11.

Bend the transformer's thick metal legs up underneath it, then solder its wire legs in holes G19, J19, M19 and H24 and L24.

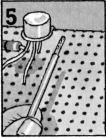

Measure the wire for two links, from C14 to J14 and from J15 to P15.

If you use stranded wire, tin the ends before soldering it to the board.*

Solder the wires in position, as shown above.

*For how to "tin", see page 148.

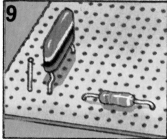

Put the yellow, violet, red resistor (4.7KΩ) in P17 and P23, then solder a short wire link from P24 to R24.

The capacitor* goes in M5 and R5 (it does not matter which leg goes in which hole). Then put the red, violet, orange resistor (27KΩ) in R8 and R14.

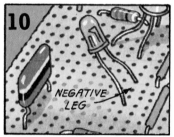

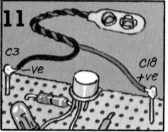

Put the LED in J12 and M12. The negative leg should be in J12. (See page 181 if you are unsure which is the negative leg.)

Solder wires for the battery to pins C3 and C18. If you use a battery clip, the black wire (negative) should go to C3, and the red (positive) to C18.

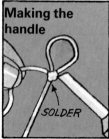

## Making the handle

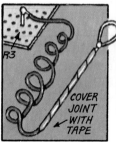

Cut a piece of tinned copper wire 10cm long. Bend the end like this. Solder.

Wind sticky tape round the handle, or cover it with the plastic sleeving.

Solder a piece of wire 1m long to the end of the handle and to pin R3.

164  *Don't worry if your capacitor looks different from this one.

## Making the metal loop

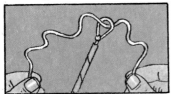

Bend the rest of the tinned copper wire to a shape like this. Then thread the loop of the handle on to it.

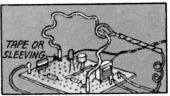

TAPE OR SLEEVING

At each end, cover about 2cm of the wire with sticky tape (or sleeving) but leave 1cm bare at the ends, for soldering. Solder the wire in holes F3 and S26.

### Loudspeaker

Now solder pieces of wire to pins H26 and L26, and solder the other ends of the wires to the back of the loudspeaker.

IF IT DOES NOT WORK, TURN TO THE FAULTS CHECKLIST ON PAGE 192

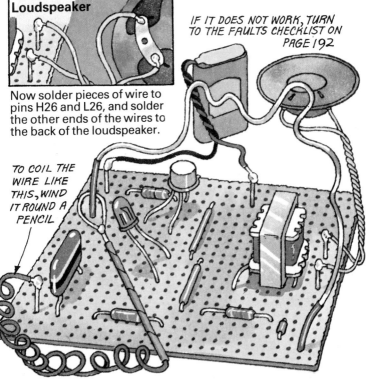

TO COIL THE WIRE LIKE THIS, WIND IT ROUND A PENCIL

Make sure all the pieces are in the right places, then connect the battery. The wire from C3 must go to the negative terminal and the C18 wire to the positive terminal.

Now, when the metal of the handle touches the metal loop, the buzzer should sound.

# Miniature radio to make

This tiny radio has only two electronic components, and it does not even need a battery. It is small enough to fit in a plastic sweet box, as shown on the right. If you want to box the radio like this, read the instructions at the end of the book before you build it.

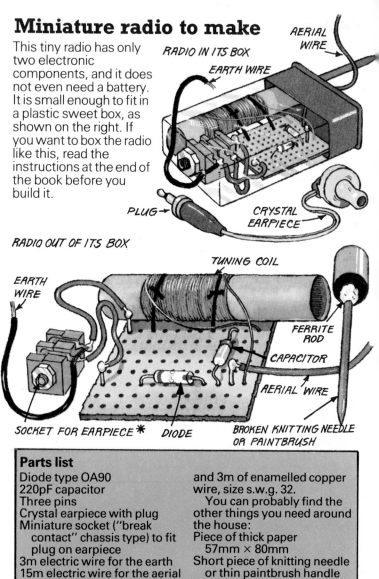

RADIO IN ITS BOX

AERIAL WIRE

EARTH WIRE

PLUG →

CRYSTAL EARPIECE

RADIO OUT OF ITS BOX

EARTH WIRE

TUNING COIL

FERRITE ROD

CAPACITOR

AERIAL WIRE

SOCKET FOR EARPIECE *

DIODE

BROKEN KNITTING NEEDLE OR PAINTBRUSH

## Parts list

Diode type OA90
220pF capacitor
Three pins
Crystal earpiece with plug
Miniature socket ("break contact" chassis type) to fit plug on earpiece
3m electric wire for the earth
15m electric wire for the aerial
Veroboard 9 tracks × 12 holes

To make the tuning coil you need a piece of 9mm diameter ferrite rod, about 10cm long, and 3m of enamelled copper wire, size s.w.g. 32.

You can probably find the other things you need around the house:
Piece of thick paper 57mm × 80mm
Short piece of knitting needle or thin paintbrush handle
"Araldite" or other strong epoxy resin glue
Paper glue and sticky tape
Thread and thin needle

*If your socket does not look like this, see page 188.

## Making the tuning coil and rod

Roll the paper once round the ferrite rod and mark where the edge of the paper first touches itself.

Cover the paper from the mark to the far edge with glue. Put the rod back on the unglued part.

Roll paper to make a tube round the rod. Make sure rod slides easily in the tube. Remove rod.

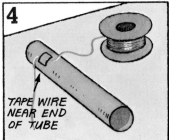

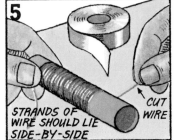

Now you have to wind the copper wire round the tube. About 8cm from the end of the wire, tape it to the tube to hold it in place.

Wind the wire neatly round the tube exactly 70 times, then cover all the wire with clear sticky tape. Cut the wire about 8cm from the tube.

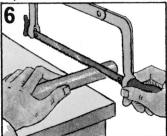

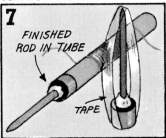

Saw a groove round the rod, 20mm from one end, then hold it in a rag and press it over a table edge to break it.*

Glue a piece of knitting needle, or paintbrush, to one end of the rod. Support it with tape for several hours until it is dry.

*Remember to wear your safety glasses.

167

## Building the circuit

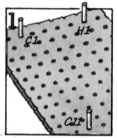

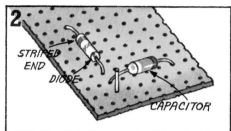

Cut the board and draw a grid with tracks vertical. Solder the pins in C1, H1 and C11.

Put the diode in holes C4 and C9, with the striped end nearest C4. The capacitor goes in holes C10 and H10, and it does not matter which leg goes in which hole.

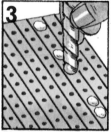

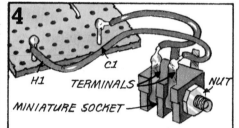

Break the track in hole C6 with a drill bit.

Now hold the socket* with the nut on the right and the terminals on top, as shown in the picture. Solder two wires about 5cm long to the two terminals nearest you. Solder the other ends of the wires to pins C1 and H1.

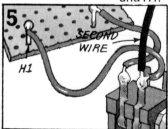

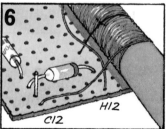

Then solder a second short wire to the socket terminal which is wired to pin H1, as shown above.

Scrape the ends of the copper wire with a knife to remove the thin coating. Solder the wires in C12 and H12. Tie tube to board using a needle and thread.

*If you have a different kind of socket, see page 188.

# Making the aerial

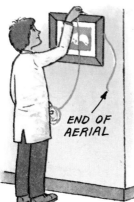

DANGLE END OF AERIAL OUT OF WINDOW

END OF AERIAL

END OF AERIAL

The aerial is a long piece of wire which picks up the radio signals. The quality of the sound from the radio depends on how good the aerial is.

To make the aerial, solder one end of the 15m electric wire to pin C11. If you live in a place with poor radio reception you may need a longer aerial. Leaving the radio where it is, unwind the rest of the aerial wire and lay it out straight. It is best if you put the free end of the aerial somewhere high, as shown in the pictures.

## 1 The earth

CROCODILE CLIP

EARTH WIRE

To make an earth for the radio, attach one end of the 3m piece of wire to a tap. You can use a crocodile clip, or strip the wire and wind it round the tap.

## 2

CONNECTION

SOCKET

Connect the other end of the earth wire to the loose piece of wire hanging from the miniature socket on the radio*

*Do not try to connect the earth wire to the earth pin in a mains plug. This is very dangerous.

## Tuning the radio

Now, if you have connected the earth and the aerial, you are ready to tune in.

TUNING ROD          AERIAL

Plug the earpiece into the socket and slide the ferrite rod into the tube. Then put the earpiece in your ear and very slowly slide the rod up and down inside the tube. You should hear several stations as you move the tuning rod.

If the sound is not very good, try moving the aerial to a different place. If the radio does not work at all, make sure all the joints are firm, check the earth connection and wiggle the earpiece plug in the socket to make sure it is firm.

## More circuits for the radio

On the next few pages you can find out how to build an amplifier and a loudspeaker for the radio.

With the amplifier you get a louder sound in the earpiece.

With both the loudspeaker circuit and the amplifier together, the sound is much louder and you do not need an earpiece.

# Amplifier for the radio

An amplifier is a circuit that makes electrical signals bigger. This is why the sound output is louder with the amplifier.

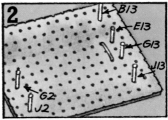

## Parts list

1.5KΩ resistor (brown, green, red)
2.7KΩ resistor (red, violet, red)
4.7KΩ resistor (yellow, violet, red)
330KΩ resistor (orange, orange, yellow)

2.2μF electrolytic capacitor
Transistor type BFY52
Chassis socket ("break contact" type) and plug
Six pins and some electric wire
Veroboard 11 tracks x 14 holes
4.5 volt battery

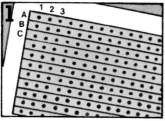

Put the Veroboard trackside up on a piece of paper. Mark a grid with horizontal tracks A-K and holes 1-14.

Turn onto the plainside. Solder six pins in holes G2, J2, B13, E13, G13 and J13. Then solder a short wire link from E12 to G12.

Next, solder the four resistors in position as shown on the right. The brown, green, red resistor (1.5KΩ) goes in B4, F4. The red, violet, red one (2.7KΩ) goes in G4, J4. The yellow, violet, red one (4.7KΩ) goes in B11, E11 and the orange, orange, yellow resistor goes in F11, J11.

*If you have a different kind of socket, see page 188.

**4**

GROOVE

The capacitor has a groove and a + sign at one end. Put the leg on that end in hole B10 and the other leg in B5.

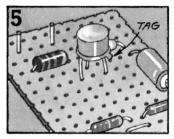

**5**

TAG

The transistor goes in holes E6, F5 and G6, and the leg nearest the tag should be in hole E6. Then break the track in holes B8 and G9.

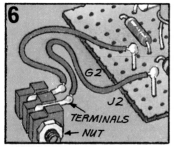

**6**

G2

J2

TERMINALS

NUT

Solder two wires to pins G2 and J2. Hold the socket* with the nut facing you. Solder the wires to the terminals on the right.

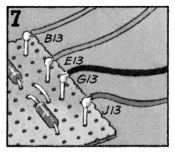

**7**

B13

E13

G13

J13

Then solder four more wires, each about 8cm long, to the four pins on the other edge of the board.

## Fixing the amplifier to the radio

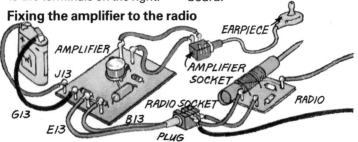

EARPIECE

AMPLIFIER

J13

AMPLIFIER SOCKET

G13

E13

RADIO SOCKET

B13

PLUG

RADIO

Unscrew the plastic case of the plug. Thread the B13 and E13 wires through the case, then solder them to the terminals on the plug. Put the plug in the socket on the radio. Connect wire G13 to the negative battery terminal and J13 to the positive terminal. Put the earpiece plug in the amplifier socket. Tune in.

*If you have a different kind of socket, see page 188.

# How to build the loudspeaker unit

If you build this circuit and connect it to the radio, you can listen to the radio without an earpiece. You will need to build the amplifier circuit on the previous two pages as well, though, as the loudspeaker unit will not work without it.

When you have built all three circuits it is a good idea to label all the wires, so you know which wire is which, and how to connect them.

**Parts list**
82Ω resistor (grey, red, black)
15KΩ resistor (brown, green, orange)
39KΩ resistor (orange, white, orange)
Two 47μF electrolytic capacitors
Transistor type AC141
Audio transformer type LT700
8Ω miniature loudspeaker
Plug to fit amplifier socket
Five pins
Some electric wire
Veroboard 13 tracks x 20 holes

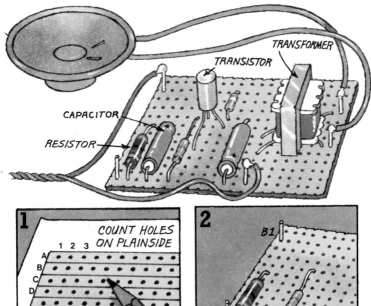

**1** COUNT HOLES ON PLAINSIDE

Draw a grid with the tracks horizontal. Solder the five pins in holes B1, M1, M13, D20 and H20.

**2**

The grey, red, black resistor (82Ω) goes in F2 and M2 and the brown, green, orange one (15KΩ) in E6, M6.

173

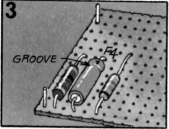

Each capacitor has a groove and a + sign on its positive end. Put one capacitor in holes F4 and M4, with the positive leg in F4.

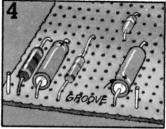

Break the track in hole M9. Put the remaining capacitor in E11 and M11, with its positive leg in M11. Then put the orange, white, orange (39kΩ) resistor in B9, E9.

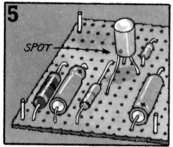

The transistor goes in E7, I7 and F9. Be careful to put the leg nearest the spot (or tag) in I7 and the centre leg in E7.

Bend the two thick legs of the audio transformer up flat under it. Then put the wire legs in B13, G13, I13, D19 and H19.

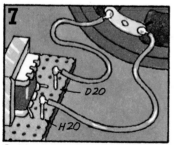

Solder two wires, about 8cm long, to pins D20 and H20. Solder the other ends of the wires to the loudspeaker.

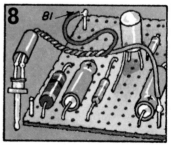

Solder two wires to pins B1 and M13. Unscrew the cap on the plug, thread wires through it and solder to plug terminals.

## Setting up the loudspeaker

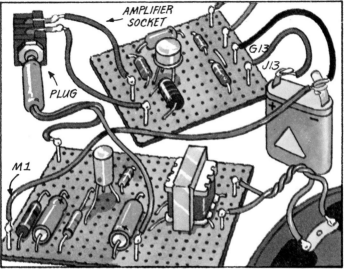

Fit the loudspeaker unit plug into the amplifier socket. Connect amplifier wire G13 to the negative battery terminal and the J13 wire to the positive terminal.

If the loudspeaker does not work, undo the cover of the plug (see picture 8) and resolder the wires the other way round.

Then connect the negative battery terminal to pin M1 on the loudspeaker with another piece of wire. Connect radio to amplifier as shown on page 172.

# More about components
# Resistors

Resistors are one of the most common components in a piece of electronic equipment. They are used to control and reduce the current in a circuit.

Inside a resistor there is a substance, usually carbon, through which it is difficult for the electrons to flow. The carbon is said to resist the flow of electrons, and this is how the resistor reduces the current.

**Fixed resistors**

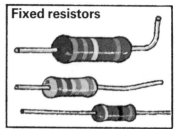

These are made with different amounts of resistance. The coloured stripes on each resistor show its value. This colour coding is explained on the opposite page.

**Variable resistors**

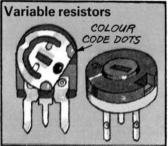

COLOUR CODE DOTS

The resistance of these resistors can be adjusted by turning the screw in the middle. They are also called potentiometers.

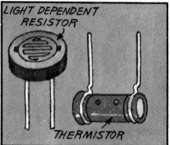

LIGHT DEPENDENT RESISTOR

THERMISTOR

A light dependent resistor has a high resistance in the dark and low resistance in the light. A thermistor changes its resistance when it is heated.

**Circuit symbols for resistors**

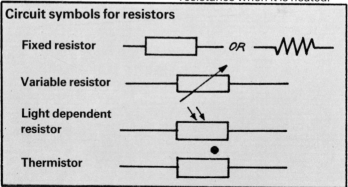

Fixed resistor    OR

Variable resistor

Light dependent resistor

Thermistor

## Resistor colour code

The three coloured stripes on one end of the resistor show its resistance. The chart on the right shows what each of the colours stands for.

Resistance is measured in ohms and the colours of the first two stripes give the first two figures in the number of ohms. The colour of the third stripe shows how many noughts you should add to the number. Each resistor also has a gold, silver, red, or brown stripe at the other end. This shows the tolerance or how accurately it is made.

| Colour | | Number or No. of 0s |
|---|---|---|
| | Black | 0 |
| | Brown | 1 |
| | Red | 2 |
| | Orange | 3 |
| | Yellow | 4 |
| | Green | 5 |
| | Blue | 6 |
| | Violet | 7 |
| | Grey | 8 |
| | White | 9 |

### Reading the stripes

COLOUR CODE STRIPES

GOLD STRIPE

Hold the resistor so the three stripes of the colour code are on the left and the other stripe is on the right. Then read the colours from left to right.

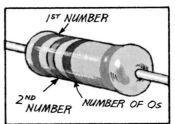

1ST NUMBER

2ND NUMBER

NUMBER OF 0s

This is a 270Ω resistor. The first stripe is red which stands for 2. The second stripe is violet which is 7 and the third stripe, brown, shows that the number has one nought.

### Variable resistor

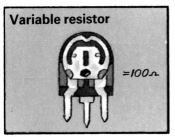

=100Ω

The maximum resistance of a variable resistor is sometimes shown by three coloured dots which you read in the same way as for fixed resistors.

### Puzzle

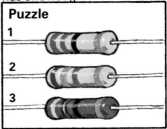

1

2

3

Can you work out the colour code on these three resistors? The answers are on the last page of this book.

# Resistor experiments

Here are some tests you can do with resistors to see how they reduce the current in a circuit. You will need a 10Ω, a 15Ω, an 18Ω, and a 22Ω resistor for the fixed resistor test, and a 100Ω variable resistor for the other test.

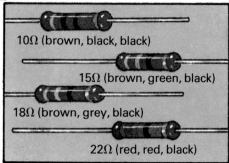

10Ω (brown, black, black)

15Ω (brown, green, black)

18Ω (brown, grey, black)

22Ω (red, red, black)

These are the resistors you will need for the fixed resistor test below.

## Fixed resistor test

For this test you need a 3.5V lamp and a 4.5V battery. Connect the four resistors to the lamp and battery as shown in the picture below. The free wire coming from the battery is called a wander lead. Touch each of the resistors in turn with the wander lead and see what happens to the light from the lamp.

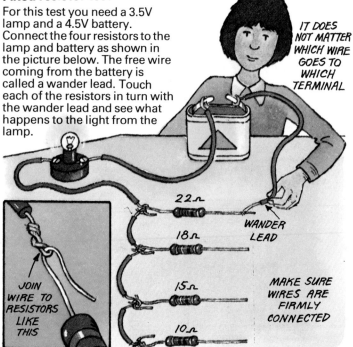

*IT DOES NOT MATTER WHICH WIRE GOES TO WHICH TERMINAL*

22Ω

18Ω

15Ω

10Ω

*WANDER LEAD*

*JOIN WIRE TO RESISTORS LIKE THIS*

*MAKE SURE WIRES ARE FIRMLY CONNECTED*

Each time you touch a resistor you make a circuit through it for the current. The bulb is dimmer with the higher value resistors because they resist the current more than the lower value ones.

## What resistors do

The current in a circuit is a bit like water in a hosepipe. If you step on the pipe you reduce the flow of the water both before and after your foot. A resistor has the same effect as your foot on the hosepipe. It reduces the flow of the current through the whole of the circuit.

## Resistor circuits

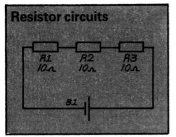

When you connect three 10Ω resistors together like this, in a series circuit, you get a total of 30Ω resistance in the circuit.

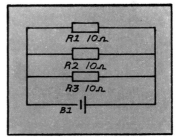

With the resistors in parallel though, there is less resistance in the circuit. With three 10Ω resistors, like this, there is only 3.3Ω resistance.

## Variable resistor test

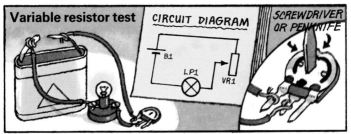

Set up the circuit as shown above, with a 4.5V battery, a 6V lamp and a 100Ω variable resistor. Join either of the wires to the centre leg of the resistor and the other wire to one of the outside legs. Turn the screw to vary the amount of resistance, and see what happens to the lamp.

179

# How diodes work

Below there are some tests you can do to see how diodes work. For these tests you need a 4.5V battery, a 6V lamp and a diode type IN4002. For the LED test on the opposite page you need a 1.5V battery and an LED

Current can flow only one way through diodes, and they always have a stripe or arrow on one end to show you how to connect them.

**Diode tests**

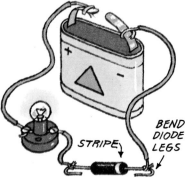

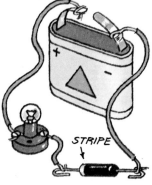

First set up the circuit as above left, with the leg on the striped end of the diode connected to the negative battery terminal. Does the lamp light up? (It should.) Then turn the diode round so the striped end is connected to the positive battery terminal, via the lamp. This time the lamp does not light up. The current can flow through the diode only when it is going towards the striped end.

**Circuit symbol**

The arrow shows which way to place the striped end of the diode.

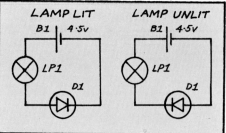

These are the circuit diagrams for the two test circuits shown above. When the arrow on the symbol points towards the negative terminal, the diode lets current flow.

## Light emitting diodes

Light emitting diodes, or LEDs, are a special kind of diode which glow like tiny bulbs. LEDs are often used in calculators to light up the numbers. Like diodes, the current can flow only one way through an LED. LEDs can have different types of negative leg.

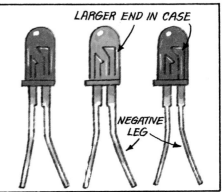

*LARGER END IN CASE*

*NEGATIVE LEG*

### Finding the negative leg

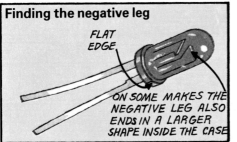

*FLAT EDGE*

*ON SOME MAKES THE NEGATIVE LEG ALSO ENDS IN A LARGER SHAPE INSIDE THE CASE*

On some LEDs the negative leg is shorter than the positive leg. On others, it is next to the edge of plastic case that is slightly flattened at the base. If you cannot recognise it, do the test below.

### Circuit symbol

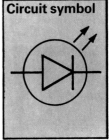

This is like the symbol for a diode, but with little arrows as well.

### LED test

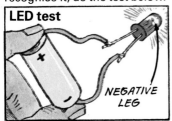

*NEGATIVE LEG*

Connect the negative leg of the LED to the negative terminal of a 1.5 volt battery. (A higher voltage will destroy the LED.) Does the LED light up?

*NEGATIVE LEG*

Then connect the wire from the negative leg to the positive battery terminal. This time the LED does not light up. Current cannot flow through it when it is connected this way.

# How transistors work

Transistors are very useful components. They can be used to control the strength of the current, and they can also act like a switch, turning the current off and on. They are one of the main components in transistor radios which are named after them.

Here is a circuit you can build to see how a transistor works. You will need a 4.5V battery, two 3.5V lamps and lamp holders and a transistor type BFY50.

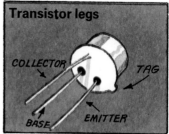

**Transistor legs**

The legs of a transistor are called "collector", "emitter" and "base". The centre leg is usually the base. You can find out how to recognize the other legs on the opposite page.

## Setting up the circuit

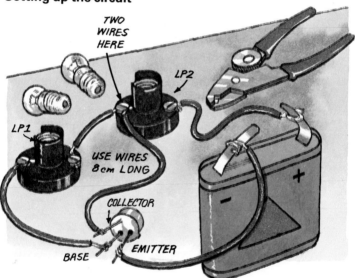

Set this circuit up very carefully and do not screw in the lamps until you are sure all the wires are connected correctly. On the BFY50 transistor, the leg nearest the tag on the case is the emitter, and it must be connected to the negative battery terminal. The base (centre leg) must be connected to lamp holder 1 and the other leg (collector) to lamp holder 2. You can fix the wires with sticky tape if you like.

## Testing the circuit

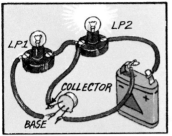

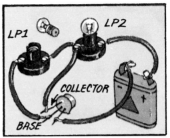

Now screw in the lamps. Lamp 1 does not light up because the current from the base leg of the transistor to the lamp is very small. The current from the collector leg to lamp 2, though, is stronger than that from the base, and lamp 2 lights up.

Try unscrewing lamp 1. There is still a circuit for the current through lamp 2 and the transistor, but lamp 2 goes out. This is because when you unscrew lamp 1, you stop the current reaching the base leg of the transistor, and this makes the transistor switch off.

## Identifying transistor legs

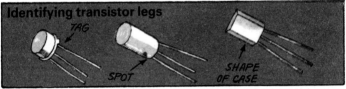

Transistors have a spot or a tag on the case, or the case may be a special shape. To identify the legs, you have to ask your supplier which leg is nearest the

mark on the case. You do not need to worry about this for the projects in this book as the instructions tell you exactly where to put the legs.

## Circuit symbols

The transistors used in this book are called junction transistors. There are two different kinds of junction

transistors and they have slightly different symbols. One kind is called "NPN type", the other, "PNP type".

**NPN type**

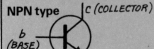

c (COLLECTOR)

b (BASE)

e (EMITTER)

**PNP type**

c (COLLECTOR)

b (BASE)

e (EMITTER)

On the circuit symbol, the legs of the transistor are labelled with their initials. On an NPN type the collector must have a

positive voltage and on a PNP type the collector must have a negative voltage.

# Boxing the projects

Here are some hints and ideas for how to box the projects. You need to decide how you are going to box a project before you build it. You may need to lengthen the legs of LEDs as shown on page 150. Also, any wires you plan to have coming out of the box need to be threaded through the box before you solder them to the circuit board. You can paint plastic boxes with acrylic or enamel paint.

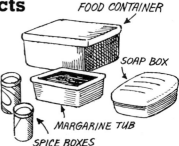

FOOD CONTAINER

SOAP BOX

MARGARINE TUB

SPICE BOXES

There are lots of suitable, ready-made boxes you can use. Plastic, wood or stiff card ones are better than tins which are more difficult to make holes in.

### Holes for wires

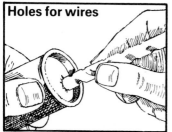

You can make neat holes in plastic or cardboard boxes with a drill bit held in your fingers. Stuff paper in the box to support it while you drill.

### Tins

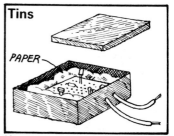

PAPER

If you use a tin, pad it with crumpled paper so the circuit board does not touch the metal. Make holes with a proper drill and smooth them with a file.

### Fixing a loudspeaker

SLOTS

If the loudspeaker is to go inside the box you need to cut slots in the lid for the sound to come out. Cut the slots with a sharp knife.

Then put strong glue on the rim of the loudspeaker and stick it over the slots, on the inside of the lid.

### 1 Miniature radio

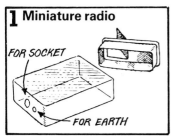

To put the radio in a box like this, make two holes in the end of the box, as shown opposite. The tuning rod and aerial wire come out of the hole in the lid.

### 2

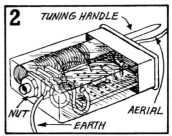

Take the nut off the socket and slide the circuit board into the box. Put the end of the socket through the hole in the box and do the nut up on the outside.

### Shaky hand game

You need to make holes in the box for the metal loop and handle. Put the ends of the loop and the wire for the handle through the holes before soldering them to the board.

### Pot plant tester

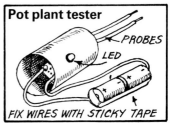

Use two small 1.5V batteries so they fit in a small box. Tape the batteries together with the positive end of one on the negative end of the other.

### 1 Guessing game

You need a hole for each of the LEDs and one for the wires for the switch. If you use a firm box, such as a soap box, you can put the switch in the lid.

### 2

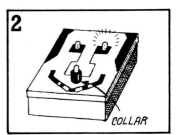

To fix the switch, unscrew the collar on the switch, put the pushbutton through a hole in the lid. Then screw the collar on again.

# Circuit diagrams for the projects

These are the circuit diagrams for the projects in this book. Each diagram shows how the components for that project are linked together. The components are labelled with their initials, number and type or value. The diagrams do not show the layout of the components on the Veroboard, only how the current flows along the tracks to each component.

## New symbols

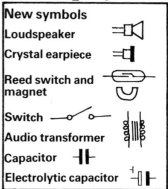

| | |
|---|---|
| Loudspeaker | |
| Crystal earpiece | |
| Reed switch and magnet | |
| Switch | |
| Audio transformer | |
| Capacitor | |
| Electrolytic capacitor | |

## Shaky hand game

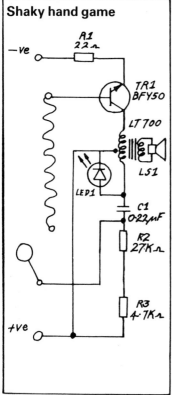

−ve

R1
22Ω

TR1
BFY50

LT700

LS1

LED1

C1
0·22μF

R2
27KΩ

R3
4·7KΩ

+ve

## Pot plant tester

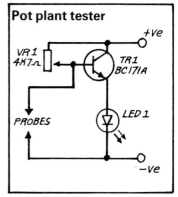

+ve

VR1
4K7Ω

TR1
BC171A

PROBES

LED1

−ve

## Miniature radio

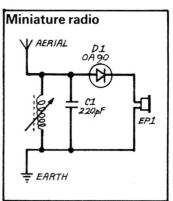

AERIAL

D1
OA90

C1
220pF

EP1

EARTH

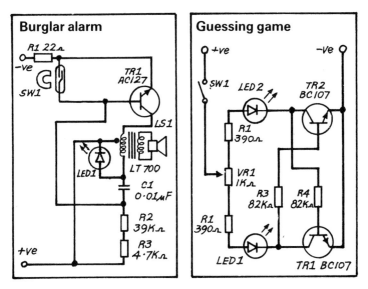

## Burglar alarm

R1 22Ω
−ve
SW1
TR1 AC127
LED1
LS1 LT700
C1 0·01μF
R2 39KΩ
R3 4·7KΩ
+ve

## Guessing game

+ve    −ve
SW1
LED 2
TR2 BC107
R1 390Ω
VR1 1KΩ
R3 82KΩ
R4 82KΩ
R1 390Ω
LED1
TR1 BC107

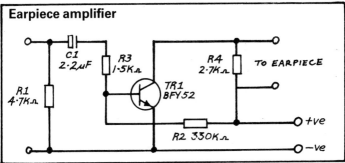

## Earpiece amplifier

C1 2·2μF
R3 1·5KΩ
R4 2·7KΩ
TO EARPIECE
R1 4·7KΩ
TR1 BFY52
R2 330KΩ
+ve
−ve

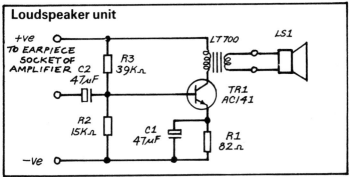

## Loudspeaker unit

+ve
TO EARPIECE SOCKET OF AMPLIFIER
C2 47μF
R3 39KΩ
LT700    LS1
TR1 AC141
R2 15KΩ
C1 47μF
R1 82Ω
−ve

# Buying components

You can buy components in an electronics components shop, or send off for them to an electronics supplier. To find the address of a supplier, look in the advertisements in electronics hobby magazines, or ask in your local T.V. repair shop. Opposite, there is a list of all the components you will need for all the projects and tests in the book, arranged by type of component (one of each of the things with a star is for the tests). If you do not want to buy all the components at once, you will need to make your own list.

## Making a list

To buy the components for only a few of the projects, copy out the parts lists given at the beginning of the projects you want to build. Check which of the things you can buy in general electrical or hardware stores (see opposite), then make a list of all the things you need to get from an electronics components supplier. Arrange your list by type of component, i.e. list all the resistors together, all the transistors, etc., and say that all the components are for use with a 4.5V or a 9V battery. State also that the Veroboard should be size 0.1in, and that you prefer "⅓ - ½ watt" resistors, and LEDs with capsule diameter 5mm.* When you go to a shop, it is a good idea to take this book with you, so they can see what you want.

## Sending away for components

If you send away for the components it is a good idea to order them all at once (it will be quite costly though), as most mail order companies have a minimum charge. Copy out the list of components very carefully. Send the list with a stamped, self-addressed envelope and the supplier will reply telling you how much the order costs. They will not send the components until you send them the money.

**Sockets**    TERMINALS

If you have a socket which looks like this, attach the wires to the two terminals as shown in the picture.

**Switch for guessing game**    TERMINALS

If your switch is not like the one in the pictures, connect the battery to one terminal, then try the wire on each of the others while pressing the switch.

*These are the best sizes for the projects, but other sizes will work as well.

# List of all the components for all the projects

## Resistors
(⅓ - ½ watt are best)

10Ω*
15Ω*
18Ω*
22Ω (three)*
82Ω
390Ω (two)*
1.5KΩ
2.7KΩ
4.7KΩ (three)
15KΩ
27KΩ
39KΩ (two)
82KΩ (two)
330KΩ

## Variable resistors
("vertical skeleton" type)

100Ω*
1KΩ
4.7KΩ

## Transistors

BC107 (two)
AC127
BFY50 (two)*
BC171A
BFY52
AC141

## Diodes

OA90
IN4002*

## Light emitting diodes
5 (any colour and size)*

## Capacitors
220pF
0.01μF
0.22μF

## Electrolytic capacitors
2.2μF
47μF (two)

## Audio transformers
LT 700 (three)

Reed switch (normally open type)
50cm tinned copper wire s.w.g. 20
3m enamelled copper wire s.w.g. 32
30cm plastic sleeving 2mm bore
10cm of 9mm diameter ferrite rod
Crystal earpiece and plug
Two miniature chassis sockets
   (break contact type) to fit plug on
   earpiece
Miniature plug to fit chassis socket
Veroboard with copper strips, size
   0.1in, sufficient for the following
   pieces (given as no. of
   tracks × no. of holes):
   13×15, 7×12, 14×30, 20×27,
   9×12, 11×14, 13×20
8Ω miniature loudspeaker (three of
   the projects need one of these –
   you can use the same one for all
   of them, or buy three)
Three battery clip connectors for
   9V battery

## Other things you need
(You can buy the things listed below in general electrical or hardware stores.)

Soldering iron
Cored solder
Very small screwdriver
Miniature pliers
Wire cutters
Wire strippers
Safety glasses
25m thin electric wire (18m of this
   is for the radio). "Bell wire"
   or stranded wire is best, but
   thicker wire will do.
Pushbutton switch
9 volt battery

4.5 volt battery ⎫
1.5 volt battery ⎪
Two 3.5 volt bulbs ⎬ for the
6 volt bulb ⎪ tests
Two miniature bulb ⎭ only
   holders
Magnet (any kind)
Clear sticky tape
"Araldite" (or other type of epoxy
   resin glue)
Paper glue
Metal paperclips (to use as
   "pins" – see page 149)

*One of each of the things with a star is for the tests.*

# Hints on identifying components

The components you buy will probably all be mixed up together and it is quite a job to identify them and work out which ones to use for each project.

The first thing to do is to sort them into different types, that is, put all the resistors together, all the transistors, etc. The pictures below should help you do this.* One or two of your components, though, may not look like any of those in the pictures. If you cannot identify them, first sort out all the rest of the components and work out which ones are for which project (there are some hints to help you on the opposite page). Then you should be able to identify the last few components by seeing which ones you are missing.

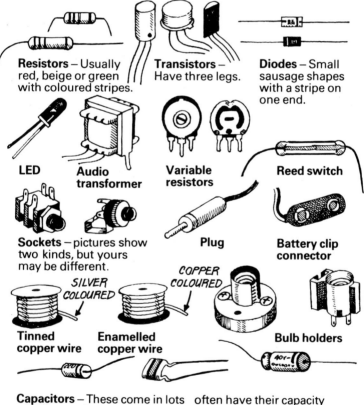

**Resistors** – Usually red, beige or green with coloured stripes.

**Transistors** – Have three legs.

**Diodes** – Small sausage shapes with a stripe on one end.

**LED**

**Audio transformer**

**Variable resistors**

**Reed switch**

**Sockets** – pictures show two kinds, but yours may be different.

**Plug**

**Battery clip connector**

SILVER COLOURED

COPPER COLOURED

**Tinned copper wire**

**Enamelled copper wire**

**Bulb holders**

**Capacitors** – These come in lots of different shapes, sizes and colours. Have two legs and often have their capacity printed on them in numbers.